Reveal that which has been hidden, she heard again. But why was it the same line? Had she sung through the whole chant again already? She didn't even remember saying the other words. And now she couldn't think of what they were. All she heard was that one line, repeated again and again in her mind. *Reveal that which has been hidden. Reveal that which has been hidden. Reveal that which has been hidden*. The voice was echoing in her head. And still something was moving beneath the water, trying to show itself to Cooper. But no matter how hard she stared, it didn't become clear.

Suddenly she heard an explosion, and the voice went silent.

Follow the Circle:

Book 1: So Mote It Be
Book 2: Merry Meet

BOOK

3

second sight

Isobel Bird

An Imprint of HarperCollins*Publishers*

Second Sight

Printed in the United States of America.
For information address HarperCollins Children's Books, a division of HarperCollins Publishers, 1350 Avenue of the Americas, New York, NY 10019.

Library of Congress Catalog Card Number: 00-104548
ISBN 0-06-447293-0

First Avon edition, 2001

❖

AVON TRADEMARK REG. U.S. PAT. OFF. AND IN OTHER COUNTRIES, MARCA REGISTRADA, HECHO EN U.S.A.

Visit us on the World Wide Web!
www.harperteen.com

CHAPTER I

She couldn't breathe.

Something was in her mouth. A rag. It tasted of dirt and oil and something else she couldn't place, like overly sweet cough syrup. Her head hurt, and a lingering chemical scent filled her nose as she tried to pull air into her lungs. She attempted to spit out the rag, but it was held there with something that wound tightly around her head. When she tried to bring her hands to her face, she found that they too, were bound.

Tape, she thought, a dim recognition flashing briefly through the haze that engulfed her mind. *It's tape.*

She tried to clear her head, to make the memories come, but the harder she tried the more confused she became. Where was she? Why was there a rag in her mouth? Why were her hands tied? She realized suddenly that she was lying on her side and that she was in a very small space. But it was dark, and she couldn't see anything. Why? Was there something over her eyes, or were they just closed? She tried blinking, and found that her eyelids didn't want to do what she asked of them. It was as if they were weighted down, shut tightly despite her fierce desire to will them open.

Finally she managed to open them a tiny bit, and even that was an enormous effort. But still she saw nothing. She was in total darkness. No light shone; there was just a fuzzy gray distortion in the blackness. Exhausted from the effort of trying to see, she let her eyes close again, almost thankfully, and concentrated on breathing. Her chest ached, and each small stream of stale air that moved through her nose brought new pain.

She knew she had to get free. But she couldn't move. Every new effort was met with resistance from the tape that circled her wrists, and she found that her ankles were also bound. She couldn't cry out for help because of the rag. And then the chemical smell came again, and she felt her thoughts becoming muddied, like the moon disappearing behind clouds. She tried one final time to breathe, and it was like hands closing around her throat.

Cooper Rivers sat up in bed, gasping. She reached for her mouth, realized that nothing was filling it and that her hands were free, and looked frantically around her. It was still night. She was in darkness, but the window across from her bed was filled with moonlight, which illuminated the familiar dresser, chair, and other contents of her room. Almost reluctantly, she let herself fall back against her pillows.

The dream had seemed so real. Even now she rubbed her wrists and moved her feet against one another beneath the sheets, making sure they were indeed free. She could feel, faintly, the tightness of the tape around her bones, and her throat was raw, as if she had been trying to breathe but couldn't.

She was afraid to close her eyes, afraid that if she did she would find that she really couldn't open them again. The sense of being trapped was still all around her. Where had she been? She tried to remember more details of the dream, but they were fading as quickly as the chemical smell that had been so strong in the dream. What had it reminded her of? For a moment the oily taste returned to her mouth, but disappeared when she swallowed, trying to place it exactly.

It was only a dream, she reminded herself. A bad dream, definitely, but still only a dream. And the strangest part was that it had come out of nowhere. Before that she'd been having a great dream, one about playing her guitar in front of a crowd at a packed club, her fingers moving over the strings while she sang the lyrics of a song she'd written. She'd been watching the mouths of the people nearest the stage moving along with hers. Then everything had gone black, and the bad dream had begun.

But now it was gone. She was breathing normally again. Her fingers rested on her chest, and she felt her heart beating. She blinked her eyes, one at a time, testing them to make sure she really could open and close them at will, and then felt ridiculous for even worrying about such a thing. Even as a little girl she had never let nightmares get to her. Dreaming had always been one of her favorite things to do, right up there with submerging herself in the bathtub and looking up through the water while she tried to count all the way to a hundred.

But she had definitely wanted this dream to end. There had been nothing fun about it. It was pure terror, and it bothered her that it had been so difficult to make it end. She had always been able to wake herself up when a dream threatened to become too frightening, and she knew she never wanted to experience what she'd just felt again. Now that she was awake, though, she was back in control.

She looked at the clock next to her bed. It was a little before six. *No sense in going back to sleep,* she told herself. It was almost time to get up anyway. She might as well work on one of her songs until it was time to get ready for school. But as she pulled the covers back and got up to get her notebook, she knew that writing wasn't the only thing that was keeping her from closing her eyes again—part of her was afraid that the dream was waiting for her to come back to it.

She wrote until the night melted away into dawn and the clear April light crept over her windowsill and spilled onto the floor. Seeing the blueness of the morning sky and the clouds going by like huge, silent sheep drove away the memory of the bad dream. She heard her father walking by her room and going downstairs to get the paper from its place on the front porch, and everything felt right again.

As she showered and dressed for the day, the dream faded from Cooper's memory. After all, she had more important things to occupy her thoughts. It was Monday, and there would be band rehearsal that night at T.J.'s house. Things had been coming together really well ever since she and T.J. had decided to put together a group. She liked the songs they were writing, and for the first time she felt comfortable showing someone else her lyrics.

Things with the Wicca study group were also going well. Ever since the dedication ceremony they'd participated in shortly after the Spring Equinox, she, Annie, and Kate had been meeting every Tuesday night at Crones' Circle bookstore with a group of other interested people to learn more about witchcraft and what it was all about. Cooper was really getting into it, and she was especially happy that she was doing it with her two friends. She'd never really had close friends like Annie and Kate before, and although the idea of being part of any kind of group was still new to her, she had to admit that she was having a lot of fun.

Grabbing her guitar case and her backpack, Cooper went downstairs. Her father, already dressed in his suit and tie, was sitting at the kitchen table, the paper spread open in front of him, while her mother looked dully into the steaming coffee cup in front of her. It always took at least two cups before her mother transformed into the perky, smiling teacher who entertained her third grade class with animated lessons that made her a favorite at the elementary school.

"Good morning, honey," she said sleepily as Cooper grabbed a muffin from the plate on the table and went to search for orange juice in the refrigerator.

"This Amanda Barclay is one tough cookie," Cooper's father said, folding the paper in half and looking at his wife and daughter over it. "If the lawyers at my firm were half as smart as she is, we'd win every case."

"Who's Amanda Barclay?" Cooper asked. "And why is she the best thing since iced coffee?"

"She's a reporter for the *Tribune*," her father answered. "She's written this investigative piece about possible corruption in the raising of funds in the last mayoral election. Really good stuff."

"Corruption in government," Cooper said. "There's a shocker."

Her father ignored her. Stephen Rivers was one of the most influential and respected lawyers in

Beecher Falls. His firm handled a lot of important clients, including some politicians. Although he didn't always know how to relate to his daughter, with her rebellious attitude and hair that changed color every other month, Cooper's father had always encouraged her to be herself. They had more in common than most people realized just by looking at them, and Cooper knew she could talk to him about anything.

Well, almost anything. She still hadn't mentioned the whole Wicca thing to her parents. They had always been generally supportive, if not entirely understanding, of her eccentricities. When she refused to go to the ballet classes her mother signed her up for when she was nine, and demanded to learn guitar instead, they let her. When she started going to concerts in rock clubs when she was twelve, they went with her, standing in the back with plugs in their ears while she danced at the front of the crowd and tried to memorize the fingerings used by the guitar players.

But witchcraft was something different. Cooper didn't know how her parents—particularly her mother—would react to the news that she had dedicated herself to a year and a day of study to decide if she wanted to become a witch. It was true that her family lived in a historic home with a reputation for being haunted by the ghost of its original owner, but still . . .

Witchcraft was something they didn't talk

about. When Cooper was a child, her mother and grandmother had spent several years not speaking to one another after Cooper's mother demanded that her mother stop teaching Cooper the little rituals and spells she'd learned in her native Scotland. Maybe it hadn't really been witchcraft Cooper was learning from her grandmother, but Cooper's mother had been frightened and angered for some reason, and they never talked about it. Because of that, Cooper had decided not to mention her interest in Wicca.

Cooper finished her breakfast in silence while her father continued to read the paper and her mother drank another cup of coffee and gradually came to life. When she was done eating, she said good-bye to her parents and left the house, walking the fifteen-minute route to school quickly. She wanted to get there a little early so she could catch T.J. before classes began. While she'd been wide awake after the nightmare, she'd worked out a problem with the lyrics to a song she'd been struggling with, and she wanted to show him what she'd come up with. At least, she thought, the dream had been useful for something.

When she arrived at school, she saw Kate sitting on the front steps with their friend Sasha, so she stopped to say hi to them before going to look for T.J.

"Enjoying the spring weather?" Cooper asked, setting down her guitar.

"Avoiding the Graces," Kate said.

Cooper grinned. The Graces were Jessica Talbot, Tara Redding, and Sherrie Adams, until recently Kate Morgan's best friends. Annie was the one who'd started calling them the Graces, because they were primarily interested in being popular and looking good, and the name had stuck. When Kate had started hanging around with Annie and Cooper, her old friends had become suspicious. Things had come to a head the month before, when another girl had seen Kate after the dedication ritual at Crones' Circle and told Sherrie about it. When Sherrie had confronted Kate and asked her if she was a witch, Kate had told her the truth. Or at least a version of the truth. She'd told Sherrie that she was friends with the owners of Crones' Circle, which as far as Sherrie was concerned was the same thing as saying she wore a pointy black hat and rode a broom.

Kate was still on speaking terms with Tara and Jessica, but she and Sherrie were definitely on the outs. And since Sherrie was the leader of the little group, Kate's interactions with Jessica and Tara were limited. To make things worse, Kate had also broken up with her football player boyfriend, Scott Coogan, at the same time she'd told Sherrie about her connection to the witches at Crones' Circle. Although everyone knew about the breakup, only a handful of people knew Kate was now dating Tyler Decklin, a guy she had met at one of the rituals the girls had attended. Scott was the star of the Beecher

Falls High School football team, and, until they'd broken up, Kate had been one of the most popular girls in school. They had been the golden couple, and Kate had been the envy of most of the girls at school.

Since the breakup, however, a lot of people had been giving Kate the cold shoulder. No one could understand why she would dump a handsome guy like Scott, particularly after he'd given up an athletic scholarship at a college in New York so that he could be closer to Kate. Scott himself had been the most bewildered, and he was still trying to get Kate to change her mind. Cooper knew that things were really tough for her friend, and although she was personally glad that Kate had chosen Tyler over Scott, she knew what it was costing Kate to do it, and what it was costing her to remain involved with the Wicca study group when it would be a lot easier for her to go back to being part of the in crowd.

"And what's going on with you?" Cooper asked Sasha.

Sasha too, was in the middle of big changes in her life. A runaway, she had come to Beecher Falls the month before, and she had met Cooper, Kate, and Annie at a Spring Equinox ritual. After some initial misunderstandings, they'd become friends, and Sasha was now living with one of the members of a local coven, the Coven of the Green Wood.

"Oh, Goddess." Sasha sighed. "So much. Social Services is looking for my parents. I guess they up and moved not long after they sent me to foster care. If nobody can find them, Thea can become my legal guardian. We're just waiting to hear."

"That would be so great," Cooper said. She liked Thea, and she knew that living with her would be wonderful for Sasha, who had bounced around from foster home to foster home since the age of seven. Sasha still hadn't told them the whole story about why she'd been given up by her parents, or what had happened to her in her last foster home to make her run away, but she seemed much more relaxed and happy now that she was out of the shelter she'd been living in. Although she wasn't part of the study group the other girls belonged to, she was interested in witchcraft and participated in the open rituals held by the local covens.

Cooper was about to excuse herself to go look for T.J. when Annie came walking up the sidewalk toward them. She looked worried about something, but Cooper figured it was just some chemistry problem she was trying to work out in her head. Of the three girls, Annie was the one with—as Kate once put it—the biggest brain. She was always interested in how things worked and why, and she approached her study of witchcraft the same way she approached a science experiment—methodically, and with a questioning mind.

"Hey," Cooper said as Annie got closer. "What's got you all worked up? Trying to figure out the molecular structure of trisodium bichloride again?"

"No," Annie said, not even smiling. She seemed upset about something. Her eyes behind the funky new glasses Kate and Cooper had picked out for her to replace the nerdy old black plastic ones she'd had when they first met were dark and serious. "Do you guys know Elizabeth Sanger?"

The other girls looked at one another, shaking their heads. "Sort of," Kate said. "I mean, I recognize the name. What about her?"

Elizabeth Sanger was a freshman, a quiet girl who kept mostly to herself. She was the kind of girl most people hardly remembered until someone mentioned her name. Cooper could kind of picture her face, but not clearly.

"She's missing," Annie answered. "She went out Saturday night to meet some friends and never got to the movie. Then she never came home. Her parents are completely freaked."

"Where'd you hear this?" Cooper asked.

"She lives on my street," Annie explained. "Her mother called my aunt to see if maybe we knew anything."

"Do they think something happened to her?" Kate asked.

Annie shook her head. "They don't know what happened. Her mother said she seemed perfectly fine when she left the house."

"Poor thing," Sasha said. "I hope she's okay." She sounded as if she was remembering her own time on the streets as a runaway, and Cooper found herself trying to imagine what that must have been like.

"Me too," Annie said. "She's a nice girl."

"Someone must have seen her somewhere," Kate said. "We'll ask around."

"Don't do that quite yet," Annie said. "Her parents are still hoping she'll just come home. They don't want anyone to panic or anything."

Cooper saw T.J. coming toward them. Picking up her guitar, she waved to her friends. "I've got something to do," she said. "I'll catch you guys later."

As she went to talk to T.J. about her lyrics, she tried again to remember exactly what Elizabeth Sanger looked like. But when she concentrated, her mouth suddenly filled with the taste of oil and dirt that she'd experienced in her dream. Shuddering, she shook her head to clear it of the memories, and by the time she reached T.J., she'd forgotten all about the nightmare.

CHAPTER 2

"Focus your attention on the water," Robin said. "Think of it as a mirror."

Cooper gazed down at the bowl she was holding in her hands. She tried to concentrate on the dark surface of the water, but it was hard. Every time she moved, even a little bit, ripples broke across the smooth surface, disrupting her thoughts. She shifted around on the cushion, took a deep breath, and tried again.

Staring at the water, she let her mind empty of all thoughts—for about two seconds. Then she found herself thinking about the way the clay bowl felt in her hands, about the new kind of incense burning on the altar at the back of the store, and how she really should set up her own Goddess altar in her bedroom. Sighing, she looked around the room to see how the others were doing. To her relief, most of them seemed to be having as much trouble as she was, judging from all the furrowed brows and frowning mouths she saw.

"It's not as easy as it sounds, is it?" Robin said.

"I guess if seeing the future was easy, everyone would be doing it," Cooper joked.

They were learning about scrying, the practice of receiving messages or information by focusing attention on a reflective surface and seeing what kinds of images came up. Robin, one of the members of the coven that ran Crones' Circle, had spent some time describing the different ways people could attempt scrying, and now she was having them try it themselves. Each person in the study group was looking into a black clay bowl filled with water and attempting to see something there.

"All I see is water," Annie said plaintively.

"That's probably all most of you will see," Robin said, laughing. "I just wanted you to get an idea of how difficult this can be. Many people think that scrying—and other magical activities—involves simply sitting down and doing it. But, like anything else you want to be good at, it takes practice and focus."

"I saw some things," said a man sitting next to Cooper. "But how do I know if what I saw was real or if they were images I made up in my head? I mean, how do I know I wasn't just daydreaming?"

"You don't always know," Robin answered. "That's what makes any divination practice difficult. You have to learn how to tell what's real from what isn't. And sometimes you still can't be sure."

"Then what's the point of doing any of it?"

asked Cooper. "If it could be that you're just making it all up, why bother?"

"What's the point of meditating?" Robin asked her.

Cooper thought for a minute. "To clear your head?" she answered hesitantly.

"Partly," Robin said, nodding. "But partly it's to change your mental state, to open yourself up to noticing what's going on around you and how these things are affecting you. In the same way, when you engage in something like scrying you're trying to open yourself up to receiving information you normally wouldn't receive because you're so busy thinking about other things and doing other things."

"So this information is always there; we just aren't always tuned into it?" Kate asked, sounding confused.

"Something like that," Robin said. "Think about dreams for a minute. All of us have had dreams, right? Sometimes our dreams are very realistic. We dream about people we know and situations we've been involved in. Other times we have dreams that seem to make no sense whatsoever, but for some reason those dreams help us solve problems we're having or make us think about things in a new way. When we dream, our minds are working in a way they can't when we're awake because we take over and make them do what we want. But when we sleep, our subconscious takes over for a while, and sometimes it shows us things we need to see.

Scrying is a little bit like dreaming while being awake."

"That still doesn't help you know what's real and what's just a weird dream," Cooper said, thinking about her own nightmare.

"That's true," Robin agreed. "And that brings us back to the original question. How do you know what to take seriously and what is just the result of eating too much sugar or not getting enough sleep? Ben, what was it you saw in the bowl?"

The man who had asked the original question looked embarrassed at being called on. "At first it just looked like swirls of colored light," he said. "But then it formed pictures. I saw myself standing in front of two doors. They were locked. I was holding a key, and I knew that it would open one of the doors. But I was afraid to try it, because I knew that behind one of the doors there was some kind of monster, and I was afraid that was the door that the key would open."

The class murmured, and Ben grinned sheepishly. "I know that sounds kind of silly," he said. "That's why I asked the question. I know there's no such thing as monsters, so I knew that what I saw couldn't be true."

"Think about the two doors for a moment," Robin said. "Do they suggest anything to you?"

"Well, sort of," Ben replied. "I thought maybe they might represent two choices."

"And are you trying to choose between two

things in your life?" Robin pressed.

Ben nodded. "And I'm kind of afraid that one of the choices might not be right for me," he said. "But I didn't need a vision to tell me that."

"Maybe not," Robin said. "But maybe this choice is more important than you think. Perhaps your subconscious is telling you to take a harder look at what's behind each of those doors before you decide which one to open."

"Okay," said Cooper. "So Ben got a message from his subconscious. But isn't scrying supposed to be used to find out about the future?"

"Sometimes it is," Robin replied. "Like I said, it's simply one way of receiving information. Different people use it differently. Ben might find scrying a useful way to sort out his feelings. You might do it and get some kind of message about something that's about to happen. Kate might do it and find herself seeing images that are coming from someone who needs to contact her from the other side."

"The other side?" Cooper said. "As in dead people?"

"It could be," Robin answered. "Don't forget—just because they're dead doesn't mean they don't have anything to say."

Cooper was confused. She had a better idea of what scrying could be used for, but she still wasn't sure how to tell if what she saw—if she ever saw anything at all—was real or not. According to

Robin, visions could come from her subconscious or her imagination. And now, apparently, they could come from dead people.

"I know you all would like there to be easy answers and easy ways of doing these things," Robin said, as if reading Cooper's thoughts. "But as we've been talking about ever since the first class, magic isn't easy. Part of being a witch is knowing when to trust your experiences and your intuition. That doesn't happen overnight. It only comes with practice, practice, and more practice. None of you are going to be able to scry right away. Some of you—maybe a lot of you—won't ever be able to do it well at all. That's okay. Everyone has different talents. As my covenmates will tell you, I, for example, am absolutely horrible at doing candle magic. I always manage to screw it up, which is why Julia will be teaching that class when we come to it. But I can scry like nobody's business, so that's why I'm the one doing this class."

Cooper wondered what her talent was. She was enjoying everything about witchcraft, but she hadn't found any one thing that she felt she could do really well. She certainly knew what she *couldn't* do well, at least not yet. She, Kate, and Annie had come together because some spells Kate had done had gone wrong. That had taught the three of them how serious working with magic could be, and it was why they were all in the class now. They hadn't tried to do any spells since those early ones. But

Cooper was getting anxious to find something she could be good at.

"The good news," said Robin, interrupting Cooper's thoughts, "is that you can't hurt anything by practicing your scrying. I'm going to teach you an easy ritual you can do. I designed it to help a person get into a receptive mode and open up to seeing and receiving whatever messages need to get through. So let's all get into comfortable positions and hold our bowls."

People moved around, some sitting on the floor and some choosing to sit on the big purple couch or in the chairs scattered around the room. Cooper crossed her legs on the cushion, sat as straight as she could, and held the bowl in her lap with her hands cupping the sides.

"Take some deep breaths," Robin instructed. "Close your eyes and feel yourself anchored to the spot. If it helps, you can use the old trick of imagining roots going down through your body and into the ground." This was a familiar way of focusing, and Cooper had done it many times. She did it now, thinking about roots connecting her with the earth, drawing up energy and filling her with light. It always made her feel more focused and more alive.

"Now I'm going to recite a quick chant," Robin informed them. "It's not exactly a spell, more like something to make your intentions clear. Just listen the first couple of times. Then, if you want to, you can say it with me." She cleared her throat and then spoke the words of the chant in a clear, strong tone: "Show me places cloaked in secrets; pierce the gloom of darkest night. Reveal that which has been hidden; let me see with second sight."

Cooper listened as Robin paused for a moment and then spoke the chant again. She tried to remember the words, so that the third time she could join in. She got most of them, but had trouble with one of the lines. But by the fourth time Robin repeated it, Cooper had it down. *It's just like memorizing lyrics,* she thought. *You just have to come up with a tune for them to help you remember.*

She did come up with a simple tune, which she played in her head as she repeated the chant to herself silently. After a minute or two, Robin told them to open their eyes and gaze into the bowl of water.

"Keep saying the chant if you want to," she said as they all stared into the bowls. "Use it to focus your thoughts."

Cooper looked at the water's surface. It was as smooth as glass. Her hands were completely still as she sat, reciting the chant over and over, waiting for something to come. She felt herself growing more and more relaxed as she sat there, and her thoughts became fuzzy as the sound of her voice in her head murmured the words. *Show me places cloaked in secrets,* she heard. The voice was hers, but there was something unfamiliar about it. It was as if someone else was singing along with her, faintly.

She listened. *Reveal that which has been hidden,* she

heard. Only this time it wasn't her own voice. It was someone else's. She looked at the water, unable to move her eyes away from it. In the depth of the bowl she thought she saw something moving. It was as if something was trying to swim up to the surface from a long way down. Something in the bowl shuddered, pushing up from the bottom.

Reveal that which has been hidden, she heard again. But why was it the same line? Had she sung through the whole chant again already? She didn't even remember saying the other words. And now she couldn't think of what they were. All she heard was that one line, repeated again and again in her mind. *Reveal that which has been hidden. Reveal that which has been hidden. Reveal that which has been hidden.* The voice was echoing in her head. And still something was moving beneath the water, trying to show itself to Cooper. But no matter how hard she stared, it didn't become clear.

Suddenly she heard an explosion, and the voice went silent. She felt something wet on her leg, and looked down. She had dropped the bowl, and the water had spilled on her jeans.

"Sorry," said a girl near her. "I didn't mean to scare anyone. I just couldn't hold that sneeze in any longer."

Robin was looking at Cooper. "Are you okay?" she asked, sounding concerned. "You were really startled."

"I'm fine," Cooper said quickly. "I guess I was

just really concentrating."

"Did you see anything?" Kate asked her.

"No," said Cooper. "No." She really hadn't seen anything. Or had she? She wasn't sure. She had definitely heard something, but it had just been a voice. *Probably my subconscious trying to sing,* she told herself.

"I think that's enough for tonight," Robin said. "If you have any questions, I can stay around for a while. Otherwise, I'll see you next week."

People got up and went to empty their bowls into the sink in the other room. Although she was wet, Cooper continued to sit on the floor. She was still thinking about the voice she had heard. For some reason, it reminded her of the dream she'd had on Sunday night. But she didn't know why. The dream had been all about her. The voice, though, didn't sound like her at all. How could the voice and the nightmare possibly be connected?

"Are you sure you're okay?" she heard Robin ask.

"Oh, yeah," Cooper said, trying to sound fine. "Just wet."

Robin smiled. "Try not to worry so much about understanding everything," she said. "Sometimes not knowing what's going on is part of the process. It just means you're growing."

Cooper laughed. "Then I must be growing a whole lot lately," she said.

Kate and Annie returned from emptying their bowls. Kate was holding hands with Tyler, who, although he was already a witch and a member of a coven, was attending the Wicca study group classes in preparation for being a teacher someday. He and Kate looked slightly awkward as they stood there, their fingers entwined.

"You two are so cute I could throw up," Cooper said, teasing them.

They both blushed deeply, and everyone laughed. "At least I didn't wet myself," Kate retorted.

"I couldn't help it," Cooper said, standing up. "I was so excited about scrying that I lost control." The sarcastic banter made her feel more like her old self, and the slightly creepy feeling that thinking about the dream and the strange voice in her head gave her retreated.

"Oh, before I forget . . ." Tyler said. "You guys know that Beltane is coming up, right?"

They all nodded. Cooper still didn't remember what all eight of the important Wiccan holidays called the sabbats were exactly, but she knew another one was about to happen.

"The coven is having its ritual on Saturday, and you guys are invited," Tyler continued. "It's going to be at Thatcher's house on the beach. We'll have a bonfire and everything. What do you think?"

"I'm in," Kate said instantly.

"Me too," Annie added.

"Sure," said Cooper. She'd had a great time at the last ritual they'd attended, the one for the Spring Equinox, and she was curious to see how this one would be different. "Does this bonfire involve roasting marshmallows and singing bad camp songs?"

"Sorry, no," Tyler said. "But I can promise you drumming and dancing, and maybe even some leaping over the fire."

"I'm definitely in then," Cooper said. "I'll wear my flameproof robe. And speaking of inviting, I have some of my own to do."

The others looked at her, surprised, and waited for her to explain herself. She hesitated. She'd actually been putting off what she had to say for almost a week. But now she had to do it.

"I'm kind of having a birthday," she said finally.

"A birthday?" Annie and Kate said loudly. "And you didn't tell us?"

"Well, birthdays aren't exactly my thing, you know?" Cooper said, trying to explain. "I didn't want to make a big deal about it."

"Excuse me," Kate said. "You're turning sixteen. That's a big deal, with a capital *B* and *D*."

"When were you planning on telling us?" Annie demanded.

"When it was all over?" Cooper said sheepishly. "But then my mom went and decided to have this birthday dinner thing. It's on Thursday. I told her you guys were probably busy, so it's okay if you don't want—"

"We're coming," Kate and Annie responded, once more speaking at the same time.

Cooper groaned. "I knew I should have lied and

told her you were both dying from the flu," Cooper said. "Fine. It's Thursday at six. Nothing fancy."

"Do boyfriends get to come?" Tyler asked hopefully.

"That would involve too much explaining," Cooper said. "Next time?"

"Okay," Tyler responded, pretending to be hurt. "But I'll have to rethink that present idea now."

CHAPTER 3

If Amanda Barclay had been any thinner, she would have been able to slide under the doors of Beecher Falls High School instead of opening them and walking through as if she owned the place, which is what she did. *But then she might have broken one of those ridiculous nails,* Cooper thought to herself as she watched Amanda take a notebook out of her bag and flip it open while she strode down the hallway, following Principal Browning as the older woman tried to get to her office.

"But Ms. Browning," the reporter said, "aren't you at all concerned that one of your students is missing? What about the safety of the others? Don't parents have a right to know?"

Principal Browning stopped so quickly that the other woman almost ran into her. The expression on the principal's face as she stared down the reporter was one of icy indignation. "Miss Barclay," she said, "of course I'm worried that one of my students is missing. But until we know exactly *why* she's missing I am not going to send the rest of the student body into a panic by suggesting that anything dire has occurred. I would appreciate it if you would do the same."

"But Elizabeth Sanger has been missing for almost four days," Amanda pressed. "Don't you think something *must* have happened to her?"

Principal Browning sighed. "What I think is that this is a matter for the police," she said sharply. "Not for a newspaper reporter. Now, if you'll excuse me, I have a lot of work to do."

The principal turned and walked away, leaving Amanda Barclay standing in the hall with her pad still hanging open. She looked annoyed as she capped her pen and returned it to her purse.

The story of Elizabeth's disappearance had been in the papers that morning. After hearing nothing from their daughter, the Sangers had gone to the police. The morning editions of the three city papers had all carried the story, as well as a photo of Elizabeth taken from the yearbook. As everyone in town now knew, Elizabeth had left home to meet her friends on Saturday night to see a movie. But she'd never arrived at the theater, and she'd never come home. According to her mother, none of Elizabeth's clothes were gone, and there had been nothing going on in her life that might make her want to run away.

"Investigators currently have no leads regarding the teen's disappearance," Annie read from Amanda

Barclay's article in the newspaper in her hand. "Anyone possessing information that might be helpful is asked to contact the Beecher Falls Police Department."

Cooper, Kate, and Annie were standing in the hall outside the art room. They had witnessed the interaction between Amanda Barclay and Principal Browning by accident, along with a dozen other students who happened to catch it while on the way to their classes. Watching Amanda in action, Cooper decided that she definitely didn't like her.

"She looks like she's never eaten anything but water and sugar-free breath mints," she said, making her friends snicker.

As if hearing Cooper's comment, Amanda turned and looked in their direction. A moment later, she was walking toward them.

"Hi," she said, flashing them a toothy smile. "I'm Amanda Barclay, from the *Tribune*. It's one of the big papers in town."

"But not the biggest," Cooper said. "Doesn't the *Monitor* have a larger circulation?"

"I suppose it might," Amanda said, her voice not quite as sweet as it had been a moment earlier. "Anyway, I was wondering if I could ask you some questions about this girl who has disappeared."

Without waiting for them to reply, she took out her pen again and made some notes on her pad. "What did you say your names are?"

"We didn't," Annie said. "And I don't see what we could possibly tell you about Elizabeth."

"Well," said Amanda, "how about telling me what she was like. Her mother said she was sort of a loner. Not many friends. Do you think she might have been depressed or antisocial or something? Did she listen to any of that goth music or anything like that?"

"Oh, please," Cooper said before she could stop herself. "I suppose you're going to say that Elizabeth must have run off because she felt alienated after listening to Marilyn Manson."

"Hey, I'm just trying to get a story here," Amanda said. "It's not like there's a lot to go on."

"Then maybe you should wait until there is," Cooper shot back.

"If you don't want to help, that's fine," Amanda said. "I'm sure I can find some students who do want to see this girl found."

"It's not that we don't want her found," Kate said. "It's just that Principal Browning is right—we don't want to upset people when we really don't know anything."

"What about boys?" Amanda asked, ignoring her. "Did she have a boyfriend? Did she date?"

"Not that I know of," Annie responded.

"And who are you?" Amanda said. "A friend?"

"A neighbor," Annie said, sounding a little intimidated by the reporter's rapid-fire questions.

"That's great," Amanda said, scribbling something on her pad. "So, did you ever see Elizabeth with anyone peculiar?"

"No," Annie said. "I never saw her with anybody. In fact, the only time I ever saw her was at school."

Amanda sighed huffily. "That doesn't really help. I need leads."

"Gee, we're sorry we can't come up with anything more exciting," Cooper said. "What's with you, anyway? You're acting like some kind of detective."

Amanda looked Cooper up and down, obviously not liking what she saw. "I'm a reporter," she said as if speaking to a child. "I report. In order to do that, I need to get the facts."

"I think we should go," Kate suggested. "We've got to get to class."

She walked away, with Annie right behind her. When Cooper didn't follow, they went back and took her by the arms, each taking one. "Come on, Cooper," Kate said. "You don't want to miss that French test."

When they were around the corner, Cooper shook them off. "I don't even take French!" she said.

"I know that," Kate said. "But I had to say *something* to get you away from that woman. You were acting like you were going to deck her."

"I'll say," said Annie. "What made you so mad?"

"I don't know," Cooper said. It was true. She didn't really know what it was about Amanda

Barclay that made her so defensive. There was just something about her. Besides, Cooper hated it when people made assumptions about other people based on their looks or the music they listened to. She herself was something of a loner. She liked to look different, and she liked music a lot of people thought was strange, and it wasn't because she hated her parents or felt alienated or anything like that, but just because she liked those things. Amanda's suggestion that Elizabeth might be disturbed because she was different had really ticked her off.

"She's just pushy is all," she said flatly.

"Hello?" Kate said. "She writes for a *newspaper*. That doesn't explain why you were so edgy. Maybe some other special day is arriving along with your birthday?"

"She really is trying to help," Annie said as Cooper pretended to slap Kate. "In her own way, I mean. Her own pushy, obnoxious, condescending way."

Cooper thought about what her father had said about Amanda Barclay at breakfast. Maybe she was a good reporter. Maybe she did know her way around a story. But she still bugged Cooper. And it annoyed her that her father found someone like that interesting.

Just then Principal Browning sent a hall monitor to escort the reporter out, and a minute later the girls heard her voicing her displeasure at being shown the door.

"I have a right to be here!" she shrieked as she was taken back to the school entrance. "This is a matter of public safety!" Her annoying voice was silenced as the doors were shut behind her.

"I guess that's that," Annie said.

But it wasn't. Amanda Barclay might have been gone, but the effect her visit had on the school grew more and more as the day progressed. Wherever Cooper went she heard people talking about Elizabeth Sanger and wondering what had happened to her.

"I heard she got mixed up in some weird cult or something," a girl said to her friend as Cooper was getting her books after third period.

"Someone told me she told a friend she had bought a bus ticket to San Francisco," said someone else while Cooper was in the line for lunch.

"I guess she left behind this note saying she was running off with some guy," a boy in her English class told anyone who would listen.

By the time the day was over, Elizabeth Sanger had hitchhiked to New Mexico, run away with a guy she'd met online, gotten caught using drugs by her parents, and become a groupie for a heavy metal band, depending on who you wanted to believe. Cooper was horrified at the things people would make up when they didn't have a single piece of real evidence to support their stories. Everyone knew someone who knew someone else who had heard the "real" story from someone he or she worked with. Suddenly, people who had probably never even spoken to Elizabeth Sanger were claiming to be her closest friends and were telling everyone their theories about where she was.

Cooper didn't know Elizabeth very well at all, but she felt sorry for her. No one had seemed to pay much attention to her when she was around, and now that she was missing the best they could do was make up wild stories about what kind of crazy person she must be. Why couldn't they just leave her alone? Probably, Cooper thought, Elizabeth had just needed to get away from people for a while in the first place. Only now, thanks to busybodies like Amanda Barclay and the kids at school, she was going to have a lot of explaining to do when she finally turned up.

Cooper went home after school and spent the evening in her bedroom, playing her guitar and working on some new songs. She thought about calling T.J. and playing him what she'd come up with, but she wasn't sure she was ready for anyone to hear it yet. She ended up playing well into the night, until she finally put the guitar down, turned out the light, and went to sleep.

Reveal that which has been hidden. The voice called to Cooper faintly, as if the person speaking the words was in another room. She herself was standing in a hallway. There were no lights on, and dark shadows slid over the carpet that ran from one end of the hall to the other. Cooper was at the top of a flight of stairs, but she couldn't remember walking up them. It was as if she'd suddenly just appeared in the house.

This time she knew she was dreaming. But everything seemed so real. She could smell the musty air, as if the house had been closed up for many years. She could see the thick layer of dust that covered the floor, and saw too the footprints that led down the hall toward the door at the other end. Was the voice coming from behind that door? Cooper listened, hoping she would hear it again. But nothing came.

Hesitantly, she walked down the hall, following the footprints. As she passed the open doorways, she looked into the rooms. The moonlight shining in the windows made everything appear as if it were under water. Cobwebs hung from the ceilings, and everything was layered with dust. But the beds were neatly made, and there were brushes, hand mirrors, and other personal items on the dressers. It was as if the people who had lived in the house had simply vanished all at once, leaving their things behind.

After passing several rooms, she came to the door at the end of the hall. The footsteps in the dust ended there. As Cooper stood in front of the door, looking at the knob and trying to decide whether or not she should go inside, she looked back down the hall. The footprints went in only one direction—into the room. There were none coming back out. That meant that whoever had made them was still inside.

She leaned forward and listened at the door. Behind it she heard muffled sounds, but she couldn't tell if they were voices or not. There were some thumps, and then the sound of something being dragged across the floor. Someone was in there. But who was it?

Reveal that which has been hidden. This time the voice seemed to come from behind Cooper. She wheeled around, looking for the speaker, but saw nothing. She peered into the gloom of the hallway, trying to make out anyone hiding in the shadows. She thought she saw something moving at the head of the stairs—not so much *someone* moving as it was a disturbance in the air there. It reminded her of looking into the depths of the scrying bowl. Something was trying to get through, but it was struggling.

More sounds came from behind the door. Cooper looked from it to the head of the stairs. What was going on? And what should she do? If the door was unlocked, she could get into the room and away from whatever it was she sensed coming at her from the other end of the hall. But another part of her was more afraid of what was behind the door, the thing making the noises.

She looked back to the stairs. There was definitely something happening there. The shadows were moving, like ripples in a pond as something surfaced from beneath the water. Cooper thought she saw something pushing against the blackness, trying to break through it. The shadows were stretching toward her, like hands reaching out for help.

As the thing in the blackness struggled, the noises behind the door grew louder. Cooper heard a series of bangs, as if someone had struck the walls, and then a long, low moan. The moans grew louder, but they were muffled, as if someone was trying to scream but couldn't.

Reveal that which has been hidden! The voice was urgent. *Reveal that which has been hidden! Reveal that which has been hidden!* The command battered Cooper again and again, the voice coming at her from many different directions. She wanted to cover her ears and block it out, but she knew that it was really coming from inside her head and that she would not be able to quiet it.

Looking up, she saw the blackness at the end of the hallway rip suddenly, and a hand appeared in the air. It was a small hand, pale and ghostly. The skin was whiter even than moonlight, and the hand hung in empty air. Cooper felt her stomach tighten as she looked at it. Where had it come from? More important—who did it belong to, and was the rest of that person about to follow?

Again the air tore, and another hand appeared. The hands reached out toward Cooper. They now ended at the elbow, and the rest of what should have been a body was swallowed by the rippling dark. Cooper stared, horrified yet fascinated, as a circle of darkness the size of a head pushed forward above the hands.

Reveal that which has been hidden! The voice was louder than it had ever been, and Cooper knew that it was coming from whatever was trying to step into the hallway from the place behind the darkness. Now one of the hands pointed at the door, a pale finger gesturing toward it anxiously.

Cooper turned away from the hands and looked at the door once more. Someone was definitely in the room behind it. She heard more thumping, and then there was a loud grunt, then a series of heavy thuds. The moaning stopped, and there was an eerie silence.

Cooper knew that she had to open the door. Despite her fear, she was sure that she had to find out what was hidden in the room. The voice had been telling her that. The thing coming through the darkness behind her was telling her that. Everything she needed to know was behind that door. She reached for the knob and turned it. It was unlocked. She pushed, and the door swung in.

"Happy birthday!"

Cooper started violently.

From her bed, she could see her mother and father standing in the doorway of her room. Her father was holding a small package wrapped in bright red paper, and her mother was standing behind him, smiling happily. Cooper wasn't in an old house. She was in her bedroom. It was morning. And she was sixteen.

CHAPTER 4

It seemed as if the man looked at the clipboard in his hand for at least an hour. While Cooper waited for him to say something, she stared out the window at the people passing by, trying to think about anything but her test results.

"Well," the man said finally, then paused for another agonizing couple of seconds during which Cooper thought she would go crazy from anticipation. "Apart from forgetting to check your rearview mirror when you backed out of the lot, you did very well."

"You mean I passed?" Cooper said.

"With flying colors," the man said. "Congratulations. You are now an official driver in the state of Washington."

Cooper was so excited she didn't know what to say. She'd been looking forward to this moment ever since she could remember. She had a license.

And even better, she had a car.

She still couldn't believe the car. A few hours

before, when her father had handed her the small wrapped box as she sat in bed, still not quite awake, she'd thought it would contain some kind of jewelry. As she'd unwrapped it, she'd tried to plan what she was going to say when it turned out to be a ring or necklace she knew she would never wear.

But when she lifted the blue velvet lid and saw the keys sitting there, she hadn't dared believe what they might mean. She just looked at her parents, unable to speak for fear that they would say something and ruin the moment.

"Want to see it?" her father had asked, and she'd practically flown down the stairs to the front door and flung it open.

There, parked in front of the house, was a car. And not just any car. Sitting on the street with the morning sun glinting off its freshly painted body was a 1957 Nash Metropolitan convertible with a white bottom half and a seafoam green top. All Cooper could do was stand on the steps staring at it, speechless.

"Where?" she'd said. "How?" Her mouth had been unable to form complete sentences.

"Your father has a client who deals in old cars," her mother told her.

Cooper had dreamed about owning a Nash Metropolitan ever since she saw one at an auto show her father took her to. She loved the two-tone paint jobs and the amber taillights. She liked the compact shape of the body and the weird way the trunk opened. She especially liked the convertibles. She pictured herself driving down the road, the wind blowing her hair back while she listened to the radio.

And now she had one. She still couldn't believe it was true. Even after she'd sat in the car and run her hands over all of the perfectly restored details, she'd half expected to wake up and find out that it was all a dream within a dream.

"Miss Rivers?"

Cooper snapped out of her daydream and looked at the man beside her. She wasn't in the Nash. She was in her father's boring old Volvo. But the Nash was waiting for her at home. She still had the keys in her pocket.

"You need to go back inside and have your picture taken for your license," the man said. He looked skeptically at her hair, which was a weird shade of lavender, the result of trying to cover the blue she'd dyed it the previous month with a new red color she'd wanted to try out. The lavender had been an accident, but she'd liked it so much she'd decided to leave it alone.

"Right," Cooper said. "Thanks."

They both got out of the Volvo and went into the building that housed the Department of Motor Vehicles. Cooper's father was sitting in a chair, looking slightly worried. When he saw Cooper he raised his eyebrows. "Well?" he said.

"You'll be happy to know that you no longer have to drive me to concerts," Cooper said.

"I don't know whether I'm happy or sad about that," Mr. Rivers replied. The truth was, Cooper was lucky to have a license at all. The state had recently changed its guidelines, upping the age at which teenagers could drive without supervision. The new rule went into effect in July, and she was thrilled that she was squeaking in under the wire.

Cooper stood in line and had her picture taken. After getting her temporary license, she and her father went home, with Cooper doing the driving.

"Thanks for letting me take the day off from school," Cooper said as they pulled up to the house. "And for taking the morning off to go with me for this."

"Hey, it's not every day you turn sixteen," her father said. "It wasn't *all* that long ago I did the same thing. Although I don't remember anyone giving me such a great car. You will let me drive it sometimes, won't you?"

"Maybe," Cooper said. "But you have to have it home by eight."

"This is the coolest car I've ever seen," Annie said.

She, Cooper, and Kate were crammed into the Nash's tiny front seat. Built for two people, it was a tight fit. But they just managed to do it. If they had to, one of them could sit sideways in the small rear space, but for now they were all up front.

"Road trips are definitely out," Kate commented from her position in the middle. "But I think I can handle going to the beach and back."

Cooper had spent most of the day looking at her car. When Annie and Kate arrived later in the afternoon, she'd bored them almost to tears by showing them every single thing and spouting endless details about the car's history. She was still going on about it almost an hour after they'd arrived.

"I haven't seen you this excited about anything but music," Kate said as Cooper showed them, yet again, how the Nash's convertible roof worked.

"You don't understand," Cooper said. "This isn't just a car. This is a piece of history. This baby was driving around the streets before my *parents* were even born. Someone could have heard Elvis Presley for the first time while riding around in it, or taken it to a drive-in to see a James Dean movie. Just think of all the things that could have happened in here."

They sat in the car for a few more minutes, until Cooper's mother came out and told them that it was almost time for dinner. Reluctantly, Cooper got out of the Nash, put the top up, and locked the doors. Then the three of them went inside for the next part of the birthday activities.

The Rivers lived in the Welton House, the former home of Frederick Welton, a trader and very bad gambler who probably would have been known as the founder of Beecher Falls, if he hadn't lost all of his land to the town's official namesake, Seymour Beecher, in a card game. The town was named after Beecher, but because the house was considered a historic landmark it was kept in immaculate condition for the tourist groups who frequently came through to look at its period furnishings and grim portraits. Whenever Annie and Kate went there, they felt like they were in a museum.

But Cooper's birthday dinner was held in the large kitchen, which was much less formal. When the girls entered the room, they found the table loaded with cartons of Chinese food.

"I'm afraid I don't have your mother's talent for cooking, Kate," Mrs. Rivers said, referring to Kate's mother's catering business, as everyone sat down. "Or yours either, Annie. I hope this is okay."

"Are you kidding?" Cooper said. "I'll take baby eggplant with garlic sauce over vegetarian lasagna any day." It was true. She did love Chinese food. But a little part of her wished that her mother didn't always buy dinners. Sometimes she thought it would be nice if they could sit down to homemade food like Annie and Kate did.

She was determined to have a good time, though, so she opened a carton and said, "Besides, let's not forget that it's *my* birthday."

"How could we?" Annie responded, taking some mu shu pork and spreading it on one of the thin pancakes it was meant to be rolled up in.

"Really," Kate said. "For someone who wasn't even going to tell us it was her birthday, you're having an awfully good time."

Cooper bit into a spring roll and waved it around as she talked. "Who wouldn't have a good time after getting both a driver's license and something to drive around in?" she asked. "And let's not forget the added bonus of getting to skip school for a day."

"Speaking of which, you picked a good day to be out," Annie said. "Amanda Barclay was back."

"Amanda Barclay?" said Mr. Rivers. "The reporter?"

Kate nodded. "She's been nosing around school ever since Elizabeth Sanger disappeared."

"What did she want this time?" Cooper asked. "I suppose she thinks one of us is hiding her or something."

"She didn't really say," Annie answered. "She was asking a lot of questions about what Elizabeth did after school and where she went and stuff like that. She came into the cafeteria during lunch and went from table to table. Finally someone told Browning, and she had her thrown out again."

"That woman never gives up," Mr. Rivers said between bites of sesame beef. "If there's a story here, you can bet she'll find it."

"Are you friends with Elizabeth?" Cooper's mother asked.

"I barely know her," Kate said. "She's a freshman. I think we had a class together once. Music or gym or something. But if we did, she never said a word."

"She lives up the street from me," Annie said. "But we weren't friends or anything. She only hung out with a few people."

"Her parents must be beside themselves," Mrs. Rivers said. "It's terrifying when a child is missing. Remember when you disappeared, Cooper?"

Annie and Kate looked at Cooper. "Something else you've never told us?" Kate asked.

Cooper rolled her eyes. "It wasn't a big deal," she said. "I ran away when I was seven." Why had her mother brought that up? She was always embarrassing Cooper by doing things like that. It was almost like she wanted people to know Cooper wasn't the perfect daughter.

"She was mad at me because I made her wear a dress to school one day," Mrs. Rivers said, looking pointedly at Cooper. "That afternoon she packed up her clothes in a little suitcase and ran away."

"Where did you go?" Annie asked.

"To the park," Cooper answered. "I was going to live in a tree."

Kate and Annie laughed, and Cooper pretended to be very interested in her shrimp dumplings. *This is exactly why I don't have my friends over very much,* she thought to herself.

"She even left a note," Mr. Rivers said. "She

said that she was leaving and that she was going somewhere where little girls didn't have to wear dresses."

"We looked everywhere for her," said Mrs. Rivers. "Finally one of the neighbors who was at the park with her two boys saw her and brought her back. Cooper was furious that she hadn't gotten away with it."

"But you never made me wear a dress again," Cooper commented.

"It's not too late," her father joked.

"It was only a couple of hours," said Mrs. Rivers seriously. "But I was really scared. I can't imagine what this girl's parents are going through."

They finished eating, and then Cooper's mother brought out birthday cake and ice cream. She turned off the lights, lit the candles on the cake, and started singing.

"Happy birthday to you," she began, and the others joined in.

Cooper looked at the candles flickering in the darkness and at the faces of her parents and her best friends, lit by the flames. Although she was embarrassed about being sung to, she was feeling pretty good about things.

"Happy birthday, dear Cooper." The voices rose up around her.

And suddenly the flames on the candles seemed to leap up in great columns of fire, forming a wall between Cooper and the people on the other side.

She was staring into an inferno blazing out of control.

For a moment she thought that maybe the curtains had somehow caught on fire. She started to leap up to find something to put out the blaze. But then she realized that there was no heat coming from the candles. She could hear the voices of Kate, Annie, and her mother and father coming from behind the flames. They were holding the last note of the line they'd been singing when the flames had suddenly grown so huge. It was as if everything had simply frozen in time.

Reveal that which has been hidden. The words flowed out of the fire, filling the room and drowning out the singing. Cooper gazed, entranced, at the flames that burned without heat. She wondered what would happen if she tried to put her hand into them, and she reached out.

A hand shot out of the flames and grabbed hers. Cooper felt the fingers close around her wrist, gripping it tightly. They were cold. The skin was pale, almost translucent, and Cooper found herself staring at the fingers. Some of the nails were broken off, with jagged edges. She thought she could see dirt streaking the ghostly flesh.

Help me. The voice sounded frightened. Cooper knew that it belonged to the person whose hand held her in its grip. Someone was in pain. In danger. Someone who wanted her to do something.

You must help me. The voice came again, insistent

and beseeching. *Reveal that which has been hidden.*

"Who are you?" Cooper spoke for the first time. Her voice sounded strange to her, as if she were shouting into a storm.

The fire shot forward, and just as she had seen something emerging from the blackness of the house in her dream, Cooper now saw that there was something pushing against the flames. The hand holding her wrist gripped even more tightly, and Cooper felt it pulling at her. The person attempting to come out of the fire was using her as an anchor.

Cooper pulled back, trying to draw the owner of the hand toward her. But something was pulling from the other side as well. Cooper was locked in a struggle with a force attempting to keep the person calling for help within the flames while she tried to pull whoever it was out of them.

Cooper wasn't scared. She was angry. She wanted to help, but someone or something was trying to stop her from doing so. She didn't know what was happening, or if it was even real, but she knew that she wanted to do whatever she could. Reaching out with her free hand, she grabbed the hand that was hanging on to her. The coldness of it soaked into her skin, chilling her.

Summoning her will, Cooper pulled as hard as she could. She felt something give way, and a figure began to emerge from the flames. The hand she was holding grew a forearm, and then an elbow. Cooper tugged again, and a face appeared in the flames. It was a girl. Her eyes were wide with fright, and she stared at Cooper in terror.

"Help me," the girl gasped. Now that she was free of the flames, her voice was clearer.

"Who are you?" Cooper asked. "What can I do?"

"Reveal that which has been hidden," she said.

Something pulled at the girl from the other side, and she began to sink back into the flames. Her eyes locked on Cooper's.

"Please," she said. "Help me."

Cooper tried to pull her back, but the force on the other side of the fire was stronger. She watched helplessly as the girl's face was engulfed in flames and her body disappeared once more into the dancing orange and red tongues. Cooper held on to the girl's hands for as long as she could, but the fingers slipped from hers, and then there was nothing but the fire in front of her.

"No!" Cooper screamed in rage and frustration. "Who are you? Come back."

There was no answer to her calls. She thought about running into the flames and trying to go after the girl. But as she stepped forward they went out, and she was staring at the candles on her birthday cake.

"Happy birthday to you." Her friends and her parents were ending the song that seemed to have begun so long ago. They looked at Cooper expectantly.

"Aren't you going to blow them out?" Annie asked. "You get to make a wish."

Cooper looked at her hand. It still felt cold where the girl had been holding it. And she could still recall the look of terror in her eyes. But what had it all meant? Who was the girl? And what had she meant when she begged Cooper to reveal that which had been hidden?

She had to tell Kate and Annie what was going on. But that would have to wait. For the moment she had to pretend that everything was fine.

Taking a deep breath, she looked at the candles on her cake. *I wish I knew what was going on,* she thought as she blew on them. One by one they went out, thin streams of smoke rising up from their blackened wicks.

"I hope your wish comes true," her mother said, plunging a knife into the cake and beginning to slice it up.

"So do I," Cooper said.

CHAPTER 5 

"She spoke to you?" Annie asked.

The three girls were up in Cooper's bedroom. After the cake and ice cream, Cooper had practically dragged them up there to tell them what had happened.

"But we didn't notice a thing," Kate said. "You were just sitting there watching us sing to you. How could all of that time have gone by?"

"I don't know," Cooper told her. "I can't explain it either. I only know what happened. And it's not the first time."

She went back to the beginning and told them the whole story, starting with her nightmare about being tied up.

"Why didn't you tell us any of this before?" Kate demanded.

Cooper shrugged. "I just thought they were bad dreams," she said. "And maybe they are."

"I don't think so," said Annie. "For one thing, this time you weren't asleep. Besides, you said you could feel how cold her hand was."

Cooper absentmindedly rubbed her wrist where the girl had touched it. "It certainly felt real," she said.

"What do you think she wants?" Kate asked.

They all looked at one another, none of them wanting to say what they were all thinking. Finally, Cooper spoke.

"I think she's dead," she said. "Why else would she look so pale?"

"None of us has actually *seen* a ghost before," Annie pointed out. "They might not necessarily look like they do in the movies."

"Cooper's seen a ghost," Kate said. "Remember? When you were little."

Cooper had, in fact, once told her mother that a strange man came to visit her in her room at night. They'd always joked that it had been the ghost of Frederick Welton and that the house was haunted. Cooper even included the story when she gave tours of the house. But now the idea of ghosts didn't seem so funny.

"I don't really remember that at all," she said. "But I'll never forget this."

"It seems strange that this all started happening around the same time Elizabeth Sanger disappeared," Kate said. "Do you think the girl was her?"

"It could have been," Cooper said. "I only saw her face for a few seconds, and mostly just her eyes. It could have been her. But it could have been any girl."

"Should we tell someone?" Annie asked.

Cooper shook her head. "What are we going to tell them?" she said. "That I've been having dreams or visions or whatever you want to call them about a girl I don't know? They're going to think I'm nuts."

"Or just upset about Elizabeth's disappearance," Kate added.

Annie frowned. "I don't think we should just sit on this," she said. "What if it *is* Elizabeth? And what if she *isn't* dead? What if she's trapped somewhere, or hurt? Maybe she's trying to get you to come look for her. Either way, this could be important."

"I need to think about it," Cooper said. "These really could be just dreams. Maybe I'll have another one tonight. But right now I don't think I'm ready to tell anyone besides you guys."

Cooper was relieved after telling her friends everything, but suddenly her perfect birthday didn't seem so perfect. Her joy over getting a car was overshadowed by her encounters with the girl. *Or with her ghost,* she thought. She felt guilty about resenting what was happening, but she couldn't help it. It wasn't like she'd tried to have the visions or anything. They'd just come to her on their own. And why her? What was it about her that made her have the dreams? When they had done the scrying exercises in class, she had been frustrated that nothing had seemed to happen. Now that things *were* coming to her, she wasn't sure she wanted them to.

"This is probably a bad idea, given what's been going on, but I got you something," Annie said. She handed Cooper a wrapped box. "I didn't want to give it to you in front of your parents."

Cooper tore off the paper and opened the box. Inside was a scrying bowl, one of the beautiful black ones they had used in class.

"I had Robin make it especially for you," Annie explained. "You seemed to like them."

Cooper looked at the bowl. The surface was smooth and shiny, and around the outer edge were inscribed the words of the scrying chant that Robin had taught them.

"It's really great," Cooper said. "Thanks."

"You don't have to use it if it freaks you out or anything," Annie said.

"No," Cooper said. "I'll use it. Maybe not tonight, but I'll use it."

"I've got a little surprise too," Kate said. She handed Cooper a second package.

The box was small but heavy. Cooper shook it, trying to figure out what might be inside. "Is it a brick?" she asked.

Kate grinned. "Something like that," she said mysteriously. "Open it and find out."

Cooper opened the box and smiled when she saw what was inside. She reached in and lifted out a small stone statue.

"It's a goddess," she said.

"It's Pele," Kate explained. "She's a Hawaiian goddess of fire. She lived in a mountain, and whenever she got angry lava would explode from it. That's how volcanoes were formed. I read about her in a book about different goddesses, and she reminded me of you. In a good way, of course. You know, you being fiery and all."

"I love her," Cooper said. "I'll put her on my altar when I actually get around to making one. In the meantime, she'll go on my dresser."

She set Pele in front of her mirror, where she looked out at the room with fierce, dark eyes. Cooper returned to the bed and sat down.

"Thanks for the presents, you guys," she said. "It's been a long time since I had an actual birthday party."

"Well, we didn't get to play pin the tail on the donkey," Kate said, "but I had a pretty good time."

"Me too," agreed Annie. "So, who has the next birthday?"

"Mine was back in January," Kate said. "Before I started hanging out with you two. You owe me one party. But I was fifteen, not sixteen, so we can make a big deal next year."

"And mine is in October," said Annie. "I guess that makes you the baby, Kate, and you the oldest, Cooper. I get to be the middle child."

"I read somewhere that most serial killers are middle children," Cooper said. "Way to go."

They talked for a while longer, and then Annie and Kate left. After her friends were gone, Cooper sat in her room and thought about what was going on. There she was, with a new car and great friends and great parents, but somewhere else Elizabeth Sanger was in trouble and her parents were home worrying about her. It didn't seem fair somehow.

And then there were the visions. Did they mean something? She was sure they did, but she didn't know what. Even she had to admit that it wasn't really like her to worry about other people, especially people she didn't even know. But being friends with Annie and Kate had changed things a little bit. She knew that she would do just about anything for them. And now she found herself wanting to help the girl in the visions. She just didn't know how.

She fell asleep, and again she dreamed. She dreamed about driving down the coast in the Nash with Kate and Annie. They were laughing and having a good time. She could smell the sea air and feel the sun on her face as they sped along, and she didn't have a care in the world.

Then one of the mountains that ran beside the road stood up, turning into a gigantic woman with long dark hair and a proud face. Cooper stopped the car and looked up at her. She knew that it was Pele and she knew this was not a dream but another vision. The goddess towered into the blue sky. She raised her hands and opened her mouth. But it wasn't words that came out. It was fire. Bright flames shot from Pele's lips, burning scarlet and orange. Pieces of molten lava fell, glowing, to the ground. Cooper knew that the goddess was angry. But angry at what? At whom?

"What do you want?" she shouted.

Pele turned her face to Cooper. Her huge eyes were like black reflecting pools. They reminded Cooper of the scrying bowls. She gazed into Pele's seemingly bottomless eyes, and in them she saw the face of Elizabeth Sanger.

"Help her," Pele said, her voice fierce as a volcano. "Help my daughter."

So it *was* Elizabeth who had been appearing to her. But what had happened to her? What did she need?

"How?" Cooper shouted. "How can I help her?"

"She will tell you," Pele replied. "Go into the fire and you will find her."

"What fire?" Cooper cried. "Where?"

But Pele was vanishing, turning once more into the mountain she had been. She sat on the earth, lifting her hands up to the sky, and her skin turned to stone. The heat of her breath was replaced by the coolness of the sea air, and everything was as it had been.

"Take a look at this," Cooper's father said when she went down to breakfast on Friday morning. He handed her the paper.

DID HE DO IT? said the headline across the front page. Below the headline was a black-and-white photograph of a confused-looking man. He was staring at the camera with a bewildered expression on his face, as if he didn't know where he was. His clothes looked dirty, and his hair was messed up, as if he hadn't cut or washed it in quite some time. Cooper quickly read the accompanying article by none other than Amanda Barclay.

> **What appears to be an important clue has been uncovered in the disappearance of Elizabeth Sanger, 15, who has been missing since the evening of Saturday, April 23.**
>
> **Following a lead from an unnamed source, the disappearance of the teen has been linked to Christopher Barrons, an unemployed handyman. Barrons, 34, sold a necklace believed to belong to Sanger to the owner of Renfield's Pawn Shop, 138 Covington Avenue. After police obtained the necklace late last evening, arresting officers apprehended Barrons at his apartment and took him in for questioning. Looking dazed as he was led away, Barrons refused to answer any questions.**
>
> **Police are not yet finished interviewing the suspect, but he appears indeed to be the man most likely to be responsible for the girl's disappearance. Not only does Barrons have**

a lengthy arrest record for crimes ranging from breaking and entering to assault, but it is believed that he was in possession of other items reported to be on Sanger's person the night of her disappearance.

Police cannot officially comment until the completion of the investigation, but Sanger's parents are convinced that Barrons is the man. "Now if they can just find her and bring her home, we can put this behind us," said a distraught Rebecca Sanger, bursting into tears at the sight of her daughter's necklace when it was shown to her. Like everyone else who has been following this case, this reporter also wishes the Sangers a quick reunion with their missing daughter.

When Cooper finished reading, she handed the paper back to her father. She didn't know what to say.

"Looks like Ms. Barclay's done it," Mr. Rivers said. "She found the guy when the police couldn't."

Cooper was shocked. "But you're a lawyer!" she exclaimed. "You know he isn't guilty until they prove it."

"I know. I know," her father said. "But you have to admit, this is pretty good evidence."

He was right. It *was* good evidence. But Cooper

didn't have to admit it. Something about the whole thing bothered her. For one thing, it didn't seem right that Amanda Barclay was writing all of those things before the police had even finished questioning Christopher Barrons. For another, it didn't fit with her own visions. Why would Elizabeth still be asking Cooper for help if her kidnapper had already been caught?

Or maybe that's what's really bothering you, Cooper told herself. *Maybe you're angry that your dreams were just dreams, and not real visions.* Perhaps, she thought, she should be happy that Elizabeth's attacker had been apprehended.

"Are you going to drive to school today?" her father asked, interrupting her thoughts.

Cooper shook her head. "It seems silly to drive when it's not that far away," she said. "Besides, I wouldn't want to make everyone jealous, would I?"

"I would," her father said, going back to the paper. "But that's just me."

When she arrived at school, Cooper was completely unsurprised to find everyone talking about the arrest of Christopher Barrons.

"I'm so glad they found him," she overheard one girl saying to another. "I was afraid to even walk home by myself."

"He looks like someone who would kidnap people," her friend responded. "Did you see those eyes? Creepy."

Cooper was amazed at how quickly people were willing to think terrible things about someone. She'd seen the picture of Barrons, and he didn't look creepy to her. Just confused.

"You'd look weird too, if someone dragged you out of bed in the middle of the night and accused you of kidnapping someone," she said to the girls as she walked away, leaving them gawking at her.

When she found Kate and Annie by their lockers, she saw that they also had the paper and were reading it.

"What do you think?" Annie asked.

"I think I wish I was still in bed," Cooper answered.

"It does seem awfully suspicious," Kate said. "If he really does have stuff that belonged to Elizabeth, that's hard to ignore."

Cooper sighed. "I had another vision," she said, and told them about Pele and what she had said.

"It *could* have just been everything we were talking about," Annie suggested. "It wasn't like Elizabeth herself was in it, like she was all the other times."

"I know," Cooper admitted. "But this felt real. I can't explain it, but I felt like Pele was telling me to do something."

The bell rang, interrupting their conversation, and they went to their different classes. For the rest of the day, Cooper listened to people talking about Christopher Barrons and Elizabeth Sanger. The more she heard, the more she wanted to believe that he really had done it. It would make things easier. A lot easier.

But something still didn't seem right. She couldn't shake the memory of how angry Pele had been, how she had insisted that Cooper do something to help Elizabeth Sanger. "Go into the fire," she'd said. If only Cooper knew exactly what she'd meant. The candles on her birthday cake had been a type of fire, and she'd had a vision looking into them. But she knew that re-creating that moment wouldn't work. Something else needed to happen.

She still hadn't thought of anything when she went home after school, turned on the television, and saw Amanda Barclay being interviewed on the news.

"I'm very pleased at the result of my investigation," she was telling a blow-dried, smiling reporter who held a microphone in front of her mouth.

The reporter turned to the camera. "There you have it," he said. "Thanks to the investigative work of journalist Amanda Barclay, Christopher Barrons has officially been charged with the kidnapping of Elizabeth Sanger. Her whereabouts remain unknown, but police are still hoping to find the girl unharmed. While many questions remain unanswered, tonight the man connected with her disappearance is behind bars, and the danger of further attacks is, we all hope, over. This is Perry Arnold for Channel Six news."

Cooper shut the television off. *No*, she thought angrily. *No, the danger isn't over. I just know it.*

CHAPTER 6

The wind rippled Thatcher's scarlet robe as he stood on the beach. His long white beard was tied with matching scarlet ribbons, and there was a crown of bright red poppies on his head. In the center of the beach a tall pole had been pushed into the sand. Scarlet, yellow, and orange ribbons hung from the top of it, fluttering in the air.

"Welcome to our Beltane ritual," Thatcher said to the people assembled around him. "I'm very pleased that all of you have come to help us celebrate this sabbat."

Cooper had almost forgotten about the Beltane gathering. In all the commotion surrounding her birthday and the disappearance of Elizabeth Sanger, the sabbat had slipped her mind. But she was glad she was there. Being with other people who were Wiccan or interested in the Craft made her feel like part of a community. Standing on the beach with Kate, Annie, Tyler, Sasha, and the other people she knew from class and from other rituals, she was able to relax a little.

"I'm sure most of you already know what Beltane is," Thatcher said. "So you can stare at the ocean or write poems in your heads or whatever you want to do while I fill in those who aren't quite as familiar with it."

Cooper laughed. She liked Thatcher. He was one of the oldest members of the Coven of the Green Wood. A carpenter, he had built the little house that overlooked the beach they were standing on. He'd lived there for many years, and holding the Beltane ritual on his land was a coven tradition. Tyler had told them all earlier that Thatcher was his godfather and that he was a wonderful storyteller. "Wait until the bonfire," he'd said. "Every year Thatcher comes up with a new story, and every year it's better than the last one."

Cooper was looking forward to that. But right now she was listening as Thatcher explained what the Beltane ritual was all about.

"We love all of the sabbats, of course," he said. "But the two that are perhaps the most popular among witches are Samhain, which celebrates the beginning of winter in the old Celtic year, and Beltane, which celebrates the beginning of summer. Our Celtic friends divided the year into two seasons, you see, and not four like we do. So these two were biggies for them."

Cooper could see why Thatcher was such a good storyteller. He used his hands and his facial expressions a lot when he spoke, and she found herself fascinated by what he was saying.

"The name Beltane has several origins," Thatcher continued. "It's a form of the Celtic and Scottish words for the month of May, for example. And it also derives from the term Bel-fire, which referred to fires lit in honor of the Celtic god Bel. Who he was exactly and what he did has gotten muddied up over the years, but basically we know that he was some kind of fertility god. So far, so good?"

People nodded and chuckled as Thatcher waited for their answers. "Good-o," he said. "That's enough of the history lesson, then. The point is, Beltane is a fertility celebration and a fire festival. Later on, when it gets dark, we'll have our bonfire. But before that—" He gestured grandly to the pole rising from the sand. "We have the maypole."

Everyone cheered at the mention of the maypole. Thatcher waited for the noise to die down, and then went on. "There are an even number of ribbons tied to the top of the pole," he explained. "There should be enough for everyone who wants to participate. Each of you will take one. But now listen up—here's the tricky part. When we begin the dance, half of you will go in one direction and half in the other. In addition to remembering which way you go, you also have to remember to go under the ribbon of the first person you meet and then let the next person go under yours."

Cooper tried to visualize the dance, but she couldn't quite get it. Neither, apparently, could a lot of other people, because there were a lot of puzzled expressions among the crowd.

"Don't worry," Thatcher said. "You'll figure it out. And it won't matter anyway, because we always manage to muck it up in the end. As long as the ribbons wind around the pole, you're doing it right. So, let's get started."

Everyone headed toward the maypole and began grabbing the ends of the ribbons. Cooper took a yellow one and walked backward until the ribbon was stretched out like a line tethering her to the pole. All around the pole other people were doing the same thing, until there was a circle of people holding ribbons. Then Thatcher held up his ribbon.

"Okay," he said. "Starting with the lovely gentleman on my left, I want every *other* person to raise her or his hand."

"When the music starts," Thatcher said. "Those of you holding your hands up will go to your right. Everyone else will go to the left. If you're *not* holding your hand up, you will go under the ribbon of the first person you meet. Then you will immediately raise your ribbon in the air while those people lower theirs, and they will go under yours. Keep doing that, and watch the magic happen."

Cooper was sure she was going to screw up. She

looked around and saw Kate and Annie looking anxiously up at the pole too. *At least I won't be the only one who looks like an idiot,* she thought as someone began drumming.

"On the count of three," Thatcher said. "One. Two. Three!"

As Cooper moved to her right, she heard a flute begin playing along with the drum. But she couldn't stop to listen to the music. She was trying to remember what she was supposed to be doing. The person to her right went under her outstretched arm, ducking to avoid hitting her. Cooper lowered her arm as the person coming toward her—Sasha—raised hers. Cooper ducked underneath Sasha's scarlet ribbon. Congratulating herself on managing to do it successfully, she almost forgot to raise her arm, but at the last minute she did, and Archer, one of the women who ran Crones' Circle, went by with a big smile on her face.

"It gets easier," Archer called encouragingly as she continued on her way.

It did get easier. After a minute, Cooper had the pattern of raising and lowering her arm and ducking under people pretty much memorized. She allowed herself to listen to the music as the dancers moved around and around the maypole in two circles going in opposite directions. She also watched as the ribbons began to wind around the maypole, crisscrossing one another and forming an intricate pattern that encased the slender pole in different colored lines.

After a couple of times around, Thatcher began singing: "Ribbons 'round the maypole go. Over, under, over, under. Ribbons 'round the maypole go, may the god our fields bless."

The others took up the song, and their voices mingled in the air like the many ribbons connecting the dancers to the maypole. Cooper danced and sang, weaving in and out among her friends. The more times they went around, the closer they got to the pole and the smaller the circle got. Eventually it became very difficult to perform the intricate process of ducking and raising their arms, and people began to lose track of where they were as their feet slipped in the sand. They tried to keep moving, but finally things got so bad that everyone was simply running around the pole in different directions, until finally they gave up and collapsed on the sand, laughing.

"Well done!" Thatcher cried from underneath a pile of bodies that had fallen on him. "Well done indeed!"

Cooper looked up at the gaily wrapped maypole. It really was beautiful. She was surprised at how something as simple as dancing and singing with other people could make her feel so good. She had never considered those things to be magical at all, but the more rituals she participated in, the more she found herself understanding the power of words and music and movement. After only ten minutes of dancing, she felt energized and filled with a sense of being part of something really magical.

The music started up again, and everyone jumped up to dance some more, this time without the ribbons. As the drumming continued, the flute began to play and other instruments joined in. Cooper found herself caught up in the general enthusiasm, and she spun and twirled around the pole with the others.

They continued to dance until the sun began to set. Then the music stopped and Thatcher motioned for them to gather around him.

"It's almost time for the Beltane bonfire," he said. "But before that, it's traditional for people to take a plunge in the ocean."

"Isn't it still too cold?" Annie asked.

Thatcher grinned. "That's the idea," he said. "It wakes you up—makes you remember what nature is all about. Then you gather around the bonfire to dry off."

He pulled his robe over his head, revealing a pair of bright red swimming trunks. Turning around, he ran toward the ocean, never pausing as he crashed through the waves and then dove into the water, disappearing for a moment and then bobbing back up with a shout.

They had all been told to wear swimsuits under

their robes or clothes. All around her, Cooper saw people getting undressed. She had worn her suit, too, and soon she was standing at the edge of the ocean, the waves tickling her feet. It really was cold, and she thought about skipping the swim.

"What do you think?" Kate asked, coming up beside her with Annie, Tyler, and Sasha.

"I will if you will," Cooper said. "All together?"

The others nodded. The five of them held hands and, shouting at the top of their lungs, ran forward, dragging one another into the water. When they were far enough out, they all dove. Cooper kept her eyes open, watching the bubbles swarm around her head as she went deeper and deeper. The cold was shocking, but it also felt good on her sun-warmed skin.

When she turned back and headed for the surface, she saw her friends all splashing around her. The setting sun was turning the waves purple and blue and pink, and it looked like they were all bobbing in a gigantic bubble bath. Cooper could see that the bonfire had been lit back on the shore.

"Let's go warm up," she called to the others, heading in.

They stumbled out of the ocean and ran for the fire. The air was cool, and they all crowded around the fire to dry off. Those people who hadn't gone swimming had gone into the house and come back out with thermoses of hot drinks. Someone handed Cooper a cup of something that smelled sweet.

"It's our special Beltane brew," Tyler informed her, noticing her hesitation as she sniffed the contents of the cup.

"What's in it?" she asked.

Tyler grinned. "That's a coven secret," he said. "You won't find out until you join. But don't worry—it's just fruit juice and spices."

Cooper took a sip of the steaming liquid. It was delicious. Plus, it warmed her up almost immediately. She wrapped herself in a towel and sat down on one of the big logs that had been placed around the bonfire. As she enjoyed the warmth of the fire on her skin, she realized what Tyler had just said: *You won't find out until you join.* Did he really think she would become part of his coven? After all, the whole point of the year and a day of studying they had all agreed to undergo was to find out if being witches was really for them.

Cooper hadn't thought much about that, but now she did. Was she going to become a witch? Would she join a coven? She, Kate, and Annie didn't really talk about that. She knew that Kate had some reservations about calling herself a Wiccan. Annie seemed less concerned about it. But still, they didn't really talk about it in any concrete way. Would she someday call herself a witch? She thought she would like to. But because of what had happened between her mother and grandmother, she had to be careful. As it was, her parents thought she was just staying over at

Annie's for the night. They had no idea that she was sitting on a beach with a bunch of witches.

She sighed. Nothing was ever uncomplicated in her life. But tonight she was determined to just enjoy herself. The sun was almost down, the bonfire was snapping, and she was with people she liked. She could sort out her worries some other time.

Thatcher, once more dressed in his scarlet robe, got up and stood beside the fire. Seeing him there, everyone stopped talking. Cooper wondered what was coming next.

Thatcher circled the bonfire, looking at the people gathered around it. "Welcome once more to this night of Beltane," he said. "As every sabbat is, this is a time for experiencing the forces of the elements. Having danced the maypole, we have felt and celebrated the powers of air and earth. In the ocean we entered the realm of water. But this is a fire sabbat, and we have saved that element for last."

He gestured toward the bonfire. "This fire is a symbol of many things," he said. "Life. Energy. Destruction and rebirth. In the flames there is great power, and tonight we have come to celebrate that power. One of the traditional Beltane celebrations was leaping the fire, passing over the flames to feel their heat and experience their power. So tonight, as we have at every Beltane ritual, we will leap the fire."

Cooper turned to Tyler, who was sitting next to her. "He wants us to jump through that?" she said doubtfully, looking at the huge bonfire. There was no way someone could jump over something that high.

"No," Tyler said. "There's a small one for this. Just watch."

Thatcher turned and pointed to the darkened beach. As he did, there was a flash of light and another, smaller fire erupted a little way down the shore. Cooper could see the shadows of people standing next to it.

"The fire is ready!" Thatcher called out. "Who will be the first to jump?"

With cheers of excitement, the people stood and ran toward the fire. Cooper went with them, gathering with Kate, Annie, and her other friends as they stopped several yards away from the smaller fire.

"How does this work?" she asked.

"You'll see," Tyler said.

Cooper watched as a woman ran toward the fire. As she reached it, she gave a loud yell and jumped, sailing over the flames and landing on the other side. The crowd cheered in delight.

Someone else ran forward and leaped the fire, the flames licking at his feet as he passed over them. Cooper stood and watched as more and more people did the same thing. Some went by themselves. Others went in pairs, holding hands as they jumped. As each person or pair went over, laughter and cheering filled the air.

It was an exciting thing to watch. The fire

wasn't particularly big or fierce, so there was little danger that someone would get burned. Still, there was something a little frightening about it, and Cooper didn't know if she wanted to take a turn or not.

Then she heard a voice in her head. *Go into the fire.* That was what Pele had said to her in her dream. Was this what the goddess had meant? It seemed to fit. But was Cooper ready to risk it? The evening had been so enjoyable. She'd almost forgotten completely about the visions, or nightmares, or whatever they were.

She hesitated, watching as several more people jumped the Beltane fire. She saw Annie run toward it and sail over, her arms outstretched and her hair flying. Tyler and Kate jumped together, Kate letting out a little shriek as they went over. Cooper knew she had to jump. Apart from whatever her dream had told her, she knew she couldn't be the only one of her friends to not leap the fire. They'd never let her forget it.

Here goes nothing, she told herself as she started running. The sand was cool under her feet as she approached the fire. She hoped she was moving quickly enough. When she got close, she bent her knees and pushed off, rising into the air. She watched as her body went over the fire, and she waited to land on the other side.

But she didn't land. Instead, she felt the now familiar sense of being awake but dreaming. The sounds of the people around her had faded away, and all she heard was the crackling of the fire. Instead of being on a beach with twenty other people, she was standing inside a ring of flames. She had entered the fire.

CHAPTER 7

"Help me."

Cooper spun around. Standing behind her was the girl from her visions, and now she knew for certain that it was Elizabeth Sanger. She was wearing jeans and a sweatshirt, and looked like any teenage girl on her way to see a movie with her friends. Except that she was as pale as milk. It was as if all the color had been drained from her body and clothes. Cooper could see the flames of the fire flickering behind her.

"Help me," she said again.

"How?" Cooper asked. "I know you need my help. But what can I do?"

Elizabeth looked at her with eyes so sad that Cooper wanted to reach out and comfort her.

"Find my body," Elizabeth said.

Cooper's heart sank. Elizabeth was dead after all. "Who was it?" Cooper asked. "Who did it? Was it Barrons?"

"I don't know," she answered. "I can't remember

that. But I know where my body is. Take them to it."

"Where?" Cooper asked. "How do I find it?"

"The house," Elizabeth said. "The one in your dreams. Look there."

"But I don't know where it is," Cooper said.

"Near the lake," Elizabeth said. "On a dirt road. I'll help you."

Elizabeth began to fade out, growing even more transparent. "I can't stay," she said. "Please, help me."

Cooper watched the girl disappear altogether. She was trying to remember everything that Elizabeth had said. A house by the lake. A dirt road. It wasn't much to go on. She wished that she had more information.

She felt a rush of hot wind, and the next thing she knew she was sprawled on the beach with the sounds of laughter in her ears. Dazed, she picked herself up and looked around. She had cleared the bonfire and was standing with the others on the other side. Kate and Annie ran over to her, smiling and laughing.

"Wasn't that fun?" Annie said. "You should have seen your face when you came over the fire."

"I bet," Cooper said.

"Are you okay?" Kate asked. "You look a little funny."

"I think I should talk to Robin," Cooper said. "Do you know where she is?"

"She's back at the big bonfire," Annie replied.

Cooper walked toward the large Beltane bonfire, with Kate and Annie following behind her. When she got there, she found Robin and some other people talking and tending to the fire while they waited for the jumpers to come back.

"Can I talk to you for a minute?" Cooper asked Robin.

"Sure," she said. "What's up?"

Cooper sat down and told her what she'd just seen in the flames of the bonfire and what had been happening for the past week. Robin listened with interest to her story, and when she was finished Cooper looked at her face anxiously.

"I know this sounds nuts," she said.

"No," Robin said. "It's not nuts at all. I think we need to talk to Thatcher and Sophia."

She stood up and motioned for Cooper to follow her. They found Thatcher and Sophia still watching the others leap the smaller fire. Robin spoke quietly to them, and they glanced over at Cooper. Cooper knew Sophia, who was part of the coven that owned Crones' Circle and who had often given Cooper, Annie, and Kate advice on their witchcraft studies, but she didn't really know Thatcher at all. Although he seemed really nice, she wondered what he would think about her story. Would he think she was making it all up? After all, she was no real witch. She was just a sixteen-year-old girl who was having some really weird experiences.

The three of them came over to Cooper. "Let's

go up to the house," Sophia said. "It will be quieter."

"What about the rest of the ritual?" Cooper asked. "I don't want to ruin it for you."

"Don't worry about that," Thatcher said kindly. "We've been doing this every Beltane for almost twenty-five years. The others know what to do."

They walked up the beach and climbed the short set of stairs that led to Thatcher's house. He led them inside to a room lined with windows that looked out on the beach. As Cooper sat down on the sofa that sat against one wall, she could see the flames of the two fires and the shapes of people jumping over the smaller of them and standing around the other.

"Robin says you've been having visions," Sophia said.

Cooper nodded. "They started last week," she said. "And they've gotten stronger. I didn't say anything because I thought I was just making it all up. But I don't think so anymore."

"And tonight this girl you've been seeing spoke to you?" Thatcher asked.

"Yes," said Cooper. "I'm sure that it's Elizabeth Sanger. She told me where to find her body. But could that really be true? I mean, it all *felt* real, but how do I know? Maybe I'm just making it all up."

"I don't think so," Sophia said. "What you've described doesn't sound like dreams or hallucinations. I think this girl contacted you on purpose."

"But why me?" asked Cooper. "I didn't even know her."

"That doesn't always matter," Robin explained. "Sometimes those who have died and need to get a message through choose someone they think will listen. You and this girl had some things in common. Maybe she felt connected to you because of that. And we were talking about scrying in class. You were thinking about the whole idea of second sight and were open to the notion. That combination of circumstances could very well have triggered these visions."

"They arrested a man in connection with the girl's disappearance, didn't they?" Thatcher asked Cooper.

"Yes," Cooper said. "But Elizabeth said she didn't know who the killer was. She said she couldn't remember. Why would that be?"

"Sometimes when people die violently, they don't remember the events leading up to it," Robin explained. "The trauma seems to erase that part of their memories. If Elizabeth really is dead, she hasn't been dead very long. She might remember the house she was in, but it's not unusual for her to have forgotten who killed her. Remembering would be too painful."

"Do you think you would recognize the house if you saw it?" Sophia asked.

"Maybe," Cooper said. "I only saw it once, during

one of the visions, and I was inside it. But I think I would be able to tell. Why?"

Sophia looked at Thatcher and Robin. "I think you need to go to the police," she said.

Cooper groaned. "Isn't there some other way?" she said.

"Not if you really want to help," Sophia responded. "Right now, they don't even know that Elizabeth is dead. Her parents don't know that she's dead. Only you do. And now we do. You have to tell someone who can help."

"But they're going to think I'm totally insane," Cooper said. "I can't just walk in there and tell them that I had these weird visions and some dead girl talked to me!"

Thatcher chuckled. "I'm not laughing at you," he said when Cooper looked hurt. "It's just that I know exactly what you mean. Most people aren't exactly open-minded about things like this. But you'd be surprised how many police departments have used psychics to help them solve cases they thought were impossible to figure out. Robin here has helped our local boys in blue out once or twice herself."

"Really?" Cooper asked, looking at Robin.

She nodded. "Thatcher's right," she said. "They won't admit that they believe in any of this, and most of them will deny ever turning to witches or psychics for help. But they'll take any information they can get, and I think they need to hear what you have to say. Can you get away tomorrow?"

"I'm happy to go with you if you want some company," Thatcher said.

"Me too," added Robin, and Sophia nodded in agreement.

Cooper thought about it. Elizabeth had come to her for help. Her parents didn't know where their daughter was. She didn't seem to have much choice. She could tell her parents she was going to spend the day with Kate and Annie.

"Okay," she said. "I'll do it."

Detective Stern looked at Cooper from across his desk. A heavyset middle-aged man with graying hair and a tired expression, he reminded her of all the detectives she'd ever seen on television cop shows, right down to the cup of coffee in his hand and the ashtray full of cigarette butts on his desk.

"You're telling me that the Sanger girl came to you in some kind of a vision?" he asked, sounding more than a little skeptical.

"We know it's somewhat unusual," Thatcher said. He had taken the red ribbons out of his beard, and looked like he could have been Cooper's grandfather.

"That's one way of putting it," the detective said. "And who are you people again?"

They had decided not to bring up the whole subject of witchcraft. Instead, they'd told the detective that they were simply people Cooper knew from a class she was taking. He had seemed to accept that at first, but now he looked at them oddly, as if trying to figure out what they were up to.

"Look," he said. "I see this a lot when kids disappear. It sets things off in other kids. They see things. They think they remember things. This Sanger girl went to your school, right?"

Cooper nodded, and the detective leaned back in his chair.

"So maybe you're dreaming about her. That doesn't mean her ghost is talking to you."

"They weren't just dreams," Cooper said, getting angry. She hated it when people didn't believe her or treated her as if she were some kind of little kid. "Some of them happened while I was wide awake."

Sophia put her hand on Cooper's arm, trying to calm her. "Have you found Elizabeth Sanger yet?" she asked the detective.

He looked uncomfortable. "No," he said. "Barrons hasn't given us anything to go on."

"Maybe because he didn't do it," Cooper said fiercely.

Detective Stern shot her a look, and she glared back at him. She'd been afraid the police wouldn't believe her, and she was beginning to regret going to them at all.

"If you don't have any leads," said Robin carefully,

"then would it really hurt to at least look into what Elizabeth told Cooper?"

"You want me to follow up clues that supposedly came from a ghost?" the man answered. "Do you know how that would make me look if I told my guys that?"

"Yeah," said Cooper. "I think I have a pretty good idea." She stood up, ready to leave, but Sophia held her back.

"You don't have to tell anyone," Thatcher said to Detective Stern. "Just take Cooper and go check it out. See if you find anything. If you don't, then no one ever knows."

Cooper watched the detective's face. He seemed to be thinking things over, weighing the possibility of embarrassing himself against maybe getting a break in the case. As for herself, she was perfectly happy for no one to know about her part in things. If the police wanted to keep things quiet, it was fine with her.

Detective Stern looked at her again, clearly trying to make up his mind. Finally, he nodded. "Okay," he said. "I give her one chance. But if she doesn't come up with anything, that's it. Let's go. My car is outside."

They stood up and left the building. Cooper got into the front of Detective Stern's car while Sophia, Thatcher, and Robin got into the back. Cooper was glad it was a plain old sedan and not a marked police vehicle. With her luck, someone would see her riding in it and start a rumor that she'd been arrested.

"I don't suppose your ghost gave you directions to this place?" the detective asked as they left the parking lot.

"Just that the house was by the lake and that it was on a dirt road," Cooper answered.

"That narrows it down to about a hundred places," Stern replied dryly.

They drove out toward the lake, located forty-five minutes outside of the city. It was a popular place for vacation homes, and there was a network of dirt roads that wound around its perimeter. As they rode along, Cooper's hopes fell. The detective was right. How would they have any idea which house to look in? Why hadn't Elizabeth been more specific? She'd said that she would help Cooper, but nothing was happening. Cooper feared that without any clear idea of where she was going, she would end up looking like the overwrought dreamer the detective had basically accused her of being.

Then, as they turned down a side road, Cooper began to taste oil and dirt in her mouth. It was the same sensation she'd had the night of the first dream, but this time she knew what it meant. Somehow, she was feeling what Elizabeth had felt as she'd been driven down the same road.

"He took her this way," she said. "Keep going."

No one asked her how she knew where to go.

They just rode in silence as they followed the road. The farther they went, the stronger the oily taste in Cooper's mouth grew. Once, when they came to a fork in the road and took the one going to the left, the taste began to fade.

"Go back," she told the detective. "I think it's the other way."

When they turned onto the right-hand road and the taste flooded her mouth, Cooper knew that she had been correct. Elizabeth was helping them find the house after all. As the fear Elizabeth had experienced surrounded Cooper, she had to remind herself that she was safe in the car with the detective and her friends.

The road went deep into the woods. After passing a few houses, they drove quite a way without seeing any more. The road became more and more bumpy, and the large ruts running through the dirt made it difficult to drive very quickly.

"This is ridiculous," Detective Stern said. "We're going into the middle of nowhere. I'm turning back."

"Please," said Cooper. "Just a little farther." The taste in her mouth was so strong that she felt she might be sick, but she knew they were close.

The detective worked the car around a fallen tree and turned a corner. There, tucked into the woods, was the house. Cooper was sure of it. Its wooden siding was weather-beaten, and the yard hadn't been tended to in a long time. It looked lonely and forgotten, and seeing it made Cooper feel incredibly sad.

"That's it," Cooper said.

Getting out of the car, she approached the front door. Detective Stern stepped in front of her. He pulled a gun from his jacket and motioned for her to get behind him.

"Just in case someone is in there," he said.

He pushed open the front door, which swung inward with a groan. In the sunlight that poured in, Cooper could see clouds of dust swirl across the floor. She could also see footprints leading from the door to the stairs beyond.

"He brought her in this way," she said. "He took her upstairs."

Detective Stern walked into the house with the rest of the group behind him. They followed him as he went quietly up the stairs, following the footprints. When they reached the top, Cooper recognized the hallway from her dream. It looked exactly the same. She looked down the hall to the door at the end.

"In there," she said, pointing. "He took her in there."

The detective walked down the hall to the door. As he reached for the knob, Cooper felt a wave of terror wash over her, and she almost collapsed. She reached out and grabbed Thatcher's arm, and he steadied her. She stood there with his arm around her, watching as Detective Stern opened the door and went inside the room.

A moment later he emerged. He looked at Cooper. "You were right," he said, sounding both surprised and unhappy. "There's a body in there, and it's Elizabeth Sanger's."

CHAPTER 8

On Monday morning Cooper made sure she got up before her parents did and retrieved the newspaper from the front steps. She wanted to see what had been written about the discovery of Elizabeth Sanger's body. The article wasn't hard to find. Once again, it was the lead story.

> **The body of 15-year-old Elizabeth Sanger, missing since April 23, was discovered by Detective Mick Stern yesterday afternoon. Acting on a tip, Detective Stern searched the area around Lake Dryer, approximately 40 miles south of Beecher Falls. Sanger's body was discovered in the bedroom of a vacation home at the remote northern end of the lake. The cause of death was not released, pending an autopsy.**
>
> **Police had already arrested Christopher Barrons, 34, earlier in the week in connection with Sanger's disappearance. Now that her body has been found, the charges against him**

will likely be upgraded to murder. Detective Stern would not confirm whether or not information provided by Barrons led to his decision to search the Lake Dryer area.

The home in which Sanger's body was found belongs to Arthur Perch, 57, the owner of a successful landscaping business. Perch reportedly has not used the home since the accidental death of his wife, Martha, there four years ago. Police sources say Perch is not suspected of any involvement in the Sanger murder, nor do they believe the two deaths are connected in any way.

There was more, but Cooper didn't need to read it. She set the paper on the kitchen table. She was relieved to see that Stern had kept his promise. Not a word had been mentioned about Cooper's involvement in helping to find Elizabeth's body. And although it bothered her that people were still assuming Christopher Barrons had killed Elizabeth, the important thing was that she had listened to the visions and done what Elizabeth had asked of her. That made her feel good. It also made her feel good to know that she had people like Sophia, Robin, and Thatcher to help her understand what was going on. She wished she could tell her parents what had happened, but she knew the time wasn't right for that. Maybe later, when she could explain her interest in witchcraft to them more clearly. But not yet.

She could, however, talk to Annie and Kate, and she hurried to school that morning to tell them all about what had happened. She hadn't been able to talk to them on Sunday night, and she knew they would be dying to know how everything went with the detective.

She was right. They practically pounced on her the minute she walked into school.

"We only have a few minutes before the bell," Annie said, dragging Cooper into an empty classroom. "Tell us everything."

Cooper tried to re-create the events of the previous afternoon as best she could for her friends. She wished she had Thatcher's storytelling abilities; everything she said sounded a lot less exciting than it had been. But Kate and Annie seemed entranced by her descriptions of the taste in her mouth and how it became stronger the closer they got to the house where Elizabeth's body was.

"I almost can't believe it really happened," Kate said when Cooper was finished with her story. "A couple of months ago, I *wouldn't* have believed it happened."

"Did you have any more dreams last night?" asked Annie.

"No," said Cooper. "I kind of thought I would. But nothing happened. I slept like a log. Robin said that sometimes when people have really strong psychic experiences like this, it takes time for the brain to recover."

"I'll use that excuse the next time I fail a math test," Kate said.

The bell for first period rang, and the girls left the room to go to their classes. Going about her regular school day activities felt strange to Cooper after what she'd been through. Everyone else seemed to have such normal lives. As she went from class to class, she looked at the faces of the other students. Apart from her, Kate, and Annie, did any of the rest of them have weird experiences they didn't tell anyone about? Were there other people seeing things they couldn't explain and thinking that maybe something was wrong with them? She wondered how unusual her visions really were, and she made a mental note to ask Robin when they had class the next evening.

Elizabeth's death was pretty much all anyone talked about, which didn't surprise Cooper at all. What did surprise her was how casually some people seemed to take it. Although a lot of students were expressing sadness, others were acting as if it wasn't a big deal—or, even worse, that it was somehow Elizabeth's own fault.

"That's what she gets for hanging out with the wrong people," she heard one guy say.

"I would never do anything as stupid as let someone take me to an old house," another girl remarked.

Such comments made Cooper angry. The people who said them hadn't seen Elizabeth's ghost. They hadn't stood in front of her and seen how sad she looked, or how frightened she'd been when she'd gripped Cooper's arm in terror. They hadn't heard the noises coming from behind the door in the house. How could they say such stupid things?

She was shaken out of her thoughts by someone tapping her on the shoulder. It was T.J.

"Hey," he said. "What's up?"

"Nothing," Cooper said, glad to see him. "Just thinking."

"Pretty weird about Elizabeth, huh?" said T.J. "I feel bad for her."

Suddenly, Cooper found herself wanting to tell T.J. everything. But she knew she couldn't. They were good friends, and they shared a love of music that she'd never shared with anyone before. But she didn't know how he would react to the news that she'd been having visions of a dead girl, let alone actual conversations with her.

"Yeah," she said, unable to think of anything else to say. "It's sad. That shouldn't happen to anyone."

"We on for practice tonight?" asked T.J. "I've got some new ideas I think you might like to go along with those lyrics you wrote last time."

"Sure," Cooper answered. "How about five at your place?"

T.J. nodded, then left for his class. Cooper continued on to hers, once again thinking about her changing life. Kate had once told her that she was afraid of becoming too involved in Wicca because it made her feel like she lived in two different worlds. Cooper hadn't really understood that, and had actually thought Kate was just making excuses because she was afraid of not being part of the popular group at school anymore. But she was starting to understand what her friend had meant.

Cooper had never been part of a popular group, so she didn't have to deal with that. But she was definitely feeling pulled in two directions. She loved her Wiccan friends, and she loved studying witchcraft. It was wonderful to be able to try different things and to talk to people who had been practicing Wicca for a long time. She was especially thrilled that she seemed to be showing some talent for the Craft. It made her feel proud, the same way writing a great song made her feel proud.

At the same time, she was finding that she had to hide her activities from more and more people. At first it had been just her parents. That was hard, but it wasn't a huge deal. After all, most kids she knew hid *something* from their parents, and it wasn't like she was doing something harmful. But now she was having to keep things from people like T.J., and she didn't like it. She wanted to be able to talk about her life with the people she trusted. But she knew from her experience with Detective Stern that a lot of people simply didn't believe in witchcraft, or at least didn't want to believe in it. Now she was afraid that other people she told might be afraid of her as well. That had never bothered her before, either. People had always been a little wary of her because she seemed so tough, and she kind of liked that. But what about people she *wanted* to get close to her? Those were the ones she was afraid of scaring off.

That evening she arrived at T.J.'s and found him in the garage, already playing. She opened her guitar case and took out the guitar, slinging the strap around her neck as she plugged the instrument into the amp.

"Where are the other guys?" she asked. Besides herself and T.J., the band consisted of a drummer whose name was Michelle—but who insisted that everyone call her Mouse—and Jed, the other guitar player. It was Jed who had come up with the band's name: Schroedinger's Cat. He was a smart guy who seldom spoke and read books Cooper had never heard of. He was always talking about things like philosophy and physics and stuff that left the rest of them shaking their heads and wondering where he came up with the things he did. He had suggested the name Schroedinger's Cat during a practice session. It was, he explained, a reference to a famous quantum physics problem involving a cat in a box and the question of whether the cat was alive or dead before someone looked into the box. The others hadn't understood a word of it, but they found the name weird enough to work, and it had stuck.

"It's just us for a while," T.J. said. "Mouse and Jed have some stuff to do, but they'll be by later."

That was fine with Cooper. Really, she and T.J. were the core of Schroedinger's Cat. They wrote the music and the lyrics. Mouse and Jed just liked playing, and were happy to do whatever the other two suggested.

T.J. was playing a great bass line as Cooper tuned up, and she stopped to listen to him. "What's that from?" she asked.

"Purely original," T.J. said, giving her a smile. "I made it up to go with the lyrics you gave me last time."

Cooper listened for a while, until she could really feel what T.J. was playing. Then she began playing something of her own over his line. She tried a few things that didn't really work, but after a while she found a melody she liked, and went with it. The two of them jammed for a while, starting and stopping as they worked out an arrangement. When they had something that hung together pretty well, Cooper decided to put her words with the music.

"Look inside me," she sang. "See my future. Tell me what it holds."

She'd written the lyrics before all of the stuff with Elizabeth had started. Singing them now, she was amazed at how well they fit the situation. It was almost eerie.

"Careful now. Don't gaze too deeply. Or you might lose your soul."

She sang the first verse again, listening to the way the words melded with the music. She liked it. T.J.'s bass line really held everything together, and the song was taking shape. As they neared what would become the chorus, she stopped playing.

"What's wrong?" T.J. asked. "Don't you like it?"

"No," Cooper said. "I love it. That's not it. I just sort of wanted to ask you something."

Ever since that afternoon, she'd been thinking about how afraid she was to talk to anyone except Annie, Kate, and her Wiccan friends about her interest in witchcraft. Now, singing her lyrics, she realized that they were all about how afraid she was to share herself with someone who might not understand.

"I'm listening," T.J. said. "Shoot."

Cooper leaned against her amp, unsure of how to begin. "How would you feel if I told you that there was something different about me?" she asked him.

T.J. laughed. "Like I don't know that already?" he said.

Cooper smiled. "I don't mean the hair or the incredible guitar playing," she said with mock arrogance. "I meant something that you don't know, that you can't tell just by looking at me."

"That could be a lot of things," T.J. responded. "Give me a hint. Is it an 'I'm the product of an alien abduction' kind of thing or an 'I'm asking Mouse to the prom' kind of thing? Because both are cool with me. You're still Cooper, right? Even if your father was from Venus. I'd be a little bummed about the prom, but only because I was sort of going to ask you myself. But it would still be okay."

Cooper paused, momentarily forgetting what she was about to say. T.J. was going to ask her to the prom? Cooper stared at him, not knowing what to think about that. Did she *want* him to ask her to the prom? She'd never really thought about it. But that would have to wait until later.

"No," she said. "Nothing like that. More of an 'I'm into something you might think is weird' kind of thing."

"Ah." T.J. nodded. "I knew you were going to confess your love of the Backstreet Boys if I just waited long enough. You're right. I can't talk to you anymore."

He wasn't making it easy for her. She wished he could be serious for just a minute. But he didn't seem to be too worried about what she was going to say, so maybe things would be okay after all. She decided to just spit it out.

"It's probably not a big deal," she began. "It's just that I've been doing something that's really important to me. And I like you." She felt herself blushing. "I mean, we're friends and all, so I kind of want you to know so that maybe we can talk about it sometimes."

She paused, trying to decide exactly how to say what was coming. For the first time, she was going to tell someone outside the Craft that she was studying Wicca. She knew she had to say it before she got too nervous. But before she could speak, the garage door opened and Mouse and Jed came in. They looked at T.J. and Cooper with puzzled expressions.

"Hey there," T.J. said. "What's with the faces?"

"Have you guys seen the late edition of the *Tribune*?" Mouse asked.

Cooper and T.J. shook their heads. Mouse opened up the copy of the paper she was carrying, and Cooper walked over to see what it said.

The headline screamed out at Cooper in letters that seemed to fill the entire front page: LOCAL TEEN PSYCHIC TOLD POLICE WHERE TO FIND THE BODY. Cooper felt a sick feeling growing in her stomach as she looked at the article beneath the words. It had been written by Amanda Barclay.

> **It has been learned that Detective Mick Stern was alerted to the location of murder victim Elizabeth Sanger's death by a local teen. Cooper Rivers, 16, reportedly went to Stern after having what sources say were a series of psychic visions in which she was given information as to the girl's whereabouts.**

Cooper stopped reading. How had Amanda Barclay found out about her? Had Stern told her? If so, why? She'd specifically asked him to not say anything. Why would he break his promise? The questions raced through her head one after the other.

She looked up and saw her bandmates looking at her. She knew they were expecting an explanation, but she couldn't give them one. Not yet. Everything had been turned upside down, and she didn't know what to do.

"I have to go," she said, throwing her guitar into its case.

"Cooper—" T.J. began.

But she couldn't look at him. All of a sudden, she knew that she wouldn't be able to handle it if he rejected her because of this. She was going to get out of there before he had a chance. She ran for the garage door and pushed it open. Before it had even shut again, she was running for home.

CHAPTER 9

"I can't believe we had to read this in the paper!" Cooper's mother was standing in the living room, waving the evening edition of the *Tribune* around, and pacing back and forth. Cooper's father was sitting on the couch, looking stunned.

Cooper didn't know what to say. She had been afraid that her parents would react exactly the way they were reacting, and she had no idea how to respond. There was a horrible silence as they stared at her and she looked at her feet.

"No one was supposed to find out," she finally said.

"Well, someone did," her mother said angrily. "And now everyone knows. The phone hasn't stopped ringing all night. I finally turned on the answering machine, and there are already a dozen messages."

"Really?" Cooper asked. "Who from?"

"Why don't you listen?" her mother said. Walking over to the answering machine, she hit the PLAY button.

"What kind of freak are you?" a male voice said before hanging up.

"Can you help me contact my father?" the second voice—a woman's—pleaded. "He died of a heart attack, and I need to talk to him. I'll pay you."

"This is Channel Eight news. Could you call us back at 555- 1362? We'd like to do a story on you."

Her mother turned off the machine. "They're all like that," she said. "Is that what you wanted?"

"I didn't want anything!" Cooper shouted. She was frustrated that her mother was treating her as if she'd done something wrong when she'd only been trying to help. "I'm sorry if I upset you. But I didn't do any of this on purpose. It just happened."

"No one said you did anything on purpose," her father said, breaking his silence. "We just wish you'd come to us first."

"Why?" Cooper said. "So you could tell me that I'm a freak, the way you did Grandma?" She hadn't meant to say it, but the words had slipped out. As soon as they had, she wished she'd kept quiet. Her mother turned and stormed out of the room.

Cooper sat on the couch next to her father. She had never cried in front of anyone in her life, but she felt like doing it now. Everything she'd feared was coming true, and all because she'd done what she'd thought was right.

Her father put his arm around her, pulling her close. "No one thinks you're a freak," he said.

"Oh yeah?" Cooper said, sniffling. "That guy on the phone does."

"Well, yes, *he* does," her father admitted. "But *I* don't. And your mother doesn't."

"I wouldn't bet on that," Cooper said. "You know what happened with her and Grandma."

"Yes, I do," said her father. "And I remember that it was very hard on everyone. But your mother feels terrible about that."

"She still doesn't want me to be weird," Cooper insisted. She couldn't bring herself to say "be a witch," even though that was what she was thinking. "And this definitely counts as weird."

"I won't deny that," replied her father. "And I won't deny that I didn't entirely understand your grandmother, or that I don't understand what happened to you. But if you say this happened, then I believe you."

"Oh, it happened, all right," Cooper said. "I couldn't make this up if I tried."

Her father sighed. "The important thing is that you helped," he said. "Which reminds me. One of the calls tonight came from Elizabeth Sanger's parents."

Cooper groaned. "What did they want?" she asked.

"There's going to be a memorial service for Elizabeth on Wednesday," he answered. "They'd like you to go."

"Do I have to?" Cooper asked. Part of her wanted to be there, but she knew it was going to be hard.

"Everyone is going to want me to talk about it."

"Things are probably going to be a little crazy for a few days," her father said. "But I think it would be a good idea for you to go. If you avoid people, it's just going to get worse."

Cooper leaned back against the cushions and sighed. "Do you ever wish you had a normal daughter?" she asked.

Her father laughed. "And miss all of this excitement?" he said. "Not on your life. But the next time you decide to talk to dead people, try to talk to one who won't get your name in the paper."

"What about Mom?" asked Cooper. "What should I do about her?"

"You'll need to talk to her," he said. "But let her cool down a little. You don't have any other surprises for us, do you? I mean, we're not going to open the paper tomorrow and find out that you're responsible for Stonehenge, are we?"

Cooper thought. Now that her parents knew about the visions, it was going to be hard to keep her involvement with the Wicca study group a secret. "Actually," she said, "there *is* something else."

It didn't take her long to tell her father about Crones' Circle and the group. She didn't mention Kate or Annie to him, because she didn't think they would want her to. She just told him that she'd been going to a witchcraft class and to some rituals.

"And these are the people who took you to the police?" he asked when she was finished.

Cooper nodded. "They're really nice," she said. "They didn't know this would happen."

"I'm sure they didn't," her father said. "All the same, I'd like to meet them. When's your next class?"

"Tomorrow night," Cooper said. "Can I still go?"

"Can I reserve my decision until tomorrow?" her father answered. "I'd like to go with you and just say hello to these people who are teaching you the dark arts." He wiggled his fingers in the air and made a ghostly noise.

Cooper rolled her eyes. "It's not like that at all," she said. "Robin and Archer and Sophia and Thatcher are just like everyone else. Well, not *just* like everyone else. But they're great. You'll see. Are you going to tell Mom about it?"

"I think I have to," he said. "But let me worry about her. You have enough to deal with. Judging from all of those phone calls, you're going to need a publicist if this keeps up."

"Should I call any of them back?" asked Cooper, thinking about the woman who wanted her to contact her dead father.

"Definitely not," said her father, hugging her. "And if anyone else asks you for anything, you tell them to call your lawyer."

Getting through the next day was incredibly hard. The minute Cooper got to school, people started asking her questions. Luckily, most of them were already afraid of her and were reluctant to actually talk to her. But some weren't, and before she'd even gotten to her first class she'd had to tell a dozen people that she wasn't going to talk about Elizabeth Sanger. The people who didn't pepper her with questions openly stared at her as she walked by.

"This is ridiculous," she told Annie and Kate at lunch. All around them, the other students were watching Cooper. Some pointed and whispered to their friends.

"They'll get over it," Annie said. "Some cheer-leader will break up with her boyfriend or some-thing and they'll move on to that."

Cooper smiled, but Kate didn't say anything. Cooper looked at her friend. "Are you okay?" she asked.

Kate put down her sandwich. "My parents read the article last night," she said.

"I think pretty much everyone in town did," Cooper answered.

"They were a little spooked," Kate continued. "They kept asking me if you talk about this stuff when we hang out, and they wanted to know what we do when we're all together. It was kind of a nightmare."

"What did you tell them?" Cooper asked.

Kate sighed. "I told them I didn't know any-thing about it. But I don't think they believed me."

"Did they say anything else?" Cooper prodded. She had the feeling that there was something Kate wasn't saying.

"They just kept talking about how dangerous it is to play with things like séances and stuff. It would have been funny if they weren't serious. But they were. I felt like I was hiding this gigantic secret from them, and I couldn't say anything."

Cooper decided she should probably tell her friends that her father was coming with her to the study group that night. She didn't want them to show up and be surprised. More important, she didn't want her father to see them and ask too many questions about what they were all doing there together.

"That's okay," Annie said after Cooper explained about her father. "I told Aunt Sarah about it too. I figured she'd find out eventually anyway."

"What did she say?" asked Cooper.

"What do you think?" Annie said. "She asked if she could come too. But I told her to find her own class."

Annie's aunt was into all kinds of things, and she believed in learning about all there was to know in the world, no matter how weird other people might think it was. It didn't surprise Cooper at all that she would be okay with Annie's studying witchcraft. Sarah herself was currently into Buddhist meditation, and they often found her sitting in the living room on her meditation cushion when they were at Annie's house.

"What about you, Kate?"

Kate looked down. "I don't think I'll be at class tonight," she answered.

Cooper and Annie exchanged a look. "Is this going to be permanent?" Cooper asked.

Kate shook her head. "I hope not," she said. "It's just that this is a little too much all at once. Especially if my parents find out. First there was the whole thing with Sherrie, Jess, and Tara, when they wondered why I stopped hanging around with them and started spending so much time with you and Annie. Then there was the breakup with Scott. You know, I've had to keep Tyler kind of a secret from them, at least the part about his being a witch. Now there's this. I don't want them to get too suspicious."

"Guilty by association, right?" Cooper said. It sounded more snappish than she'd intended, and Kate looked hurt.

"I can't help it if my parents are a little more conservative than your father is or Annie's aunt is," she said, sounding hurt. "They understand a lot, but they wouldn't understand this."

"I didn't mean it that way," Cooper said. "I'm sorry. It's just that I hate feeling like some kind of carnival attraction."

"I just think I should lie low for a little bit," Kate said. "It's not like I'm going to stop eating lunch with you or stop hanging out with you or anything. I have learned *something* from all of this."

"I know," Cooper said. "And I really do understand. I'm lucky my dad didn't totally flip out. My mom is another story."

As she spoke, she noticed that T.J. was walking toward their table. "Oh, great," she said. "Just what I need."

T.J. came up and nodded at Annie and Kate, who greeted him. He reached into his shirt pocket and pulled out something that he handed to Cooper.

"What's this?" she asked.

"A tape," he said. "Of our song. We made it after you left last night. I tried to teach Jed the stuff you were playing, but I don't think I got it right. Still, I think it sounds pretty good. See what you think. If you like it, we can record it again next week with your vocals."

Cooper didn't know how to respond. She knew that this was T.J.'s way of saying that everything was cool between them. She felt a big chunk of the anxiety that had taken up residence in her chest break up and drift away.

"Thanks," she said. "Thanks a lot. I can't wait to hear it."

T.J. waved good-bye and walked off, leaving them alone. Cooper watched him go, once more amazed at how important it was to her that he still liked her and wanted to be her friend.

"See," Annie said, noticing Cooper's reaction. "Not everyone is afraid of you."

Cooper didn't say anything. She just put the tape in her pocket.

* * *

Cooper and her father arrived at Crones' Circle about half an hour before the class was supposed to start. Cooper had phoned ahead and asked Sophia if it was all right to bring him, and Sophia had enthusiastically supported the idea. When Cooper came in with her father in tow, Sophia walked over and greeted them warmly.

"It's so nice to meet you," she said, taking Mr. Rivers's hand in both of hers. "We all love having Cooper here."

"From what she tells me, she likes being here," he responded.

Sophia guided him to the back room of the store, where it was more private. She gestured for him to take a seat in one of the chairs.

"I really don't know what to say," Mr. Rivers said after sitting. "I guess I really just wanted to find out what Cooper has gotten herself into."

Sophia smiled. "That's entirely understandable," she said. "A lot of people are apprehensive when they hear about anything to do with Wicca."

"I know a little about it," Cooper's father said. "But not a great deal. You can imagine that it was something of a surprise to read about Cooper's experiences in the paper."

Sophia frowned. "We're very disturbed by that," she said. "It was a great breach of trust on the part of someone in the police department. Thatcher is trying to find out what happened."

As if on cue, Thatcher walked into the room.

When Cooper's father saw him, he looked startled. "Thatcher Morris?" he said. "*You're* the Thatcher I keep hearing about?"

"Stephen Rivers," Thatcher said, sounding equally surprised. "You mean this is *your* little girl? I had no idea."

The two men shook hands while Cooper and Sophia looked at one another, neither knowing what to think.

"You two know each other?" Cooper asked in disbelief.

"Thatcher did the carpentry work on my offices a few years ago," Mr. Rivers said.

"And a damn fine job I did too," Thatcher added.

Mr. Rivers shook his head. "This just gets stranger and stranger. Is everyone around here into this Wicca business except me?"

"We didn't want to tell you," Thatcher said. "But yes, you're the only one who isn't." He laughed loudly, then paused. "Seriously, Stephen, this child of yours has some strong talent. I hope you'll consider letting her study with us and see if it's something she wants to develop."

Mr. Rivers looked at Cooper. "It's really her mother who worries," he said. "There's some family history there, as Cooper might have told you."

"We don't want to do anything that might be against a parent's wishes," Sophia said. "If you'd prefer Cooper didn't come, then we'll respect that."

Cooper held her breath. If her father said she

couldn't continue coming to the study group, she knew Sophia would abide by his decision. She also knew that it would be very tempting for him to say no. It would make her mother happy, and it would be easier for everyone. Except for her. She very badly wanted to remain in the group, and not just because her friends were in it. She'd come to feel very connected to witchcraft, and she wanted to deepen that connection. She figured she could do some of it on her own, but she knew that practicing with other people was very important. She waited anxiously to hear what her father's verdict was going to be.

"Well," he said slowly, "as I said, I don't really get what all of this is about. But Cooper seems to be in good hands. I don't see why she shouldn't stay in them."

CHAPTER 10

The memorial for Elizabeth Sanger was held at the synagogue her family attended. The sanctuary was filled with white lilies, and the pews were filled with friends and family members who had come to say good-bye to the dead girl. Following Jewish tradition, the service for the family and the actual funeral had been held the day following the discovery of Elizabeth's body. But so many people had followed the story of her disappearance that the family had decided to hold another service for those who had been unable to attend the first one.

Cooper entered the synagogue accompanied by Kate and Annie. The school had excused anyone who wanted to attend the service, and Cooper noted bitterly that a lot of people who probably had never even spoken to Elizabeth Sanger had decided to take advantage of the occasion. As she and her friends took a place in one of the pews, she scanned the crowd, looking for familiar faces.

"I bet more than half these people are here just

to get out of class," she muttered. "They didn't even know her."

Cooper had waited until the last minute before deciding to come. Despite the message from the Sangers, she wasn't sure she would be welcome there. She *had* listened to the messages on her family's answering machine, and a lot of them had been hostile, even threatening. She couldn't understand why so many people seemed to think that her visions were something to fear.

As they waited for the service to begin, a woman came over and sat beside Cooper. The woman was thin and looked very nervous. She wore a plain black dress, and it was obvious that she had been crying.

"I'm Rebecca Sanger," she said.

Cooper tensed up. She didn't know what to say to Elizabeth's mother. All she could do was nod.

"I don't know why you saw what you did," Mrs. Sanger said carefully. "I don't really understand it. But I wanted to thank you for helping us find our little girl."

Mrs. Sanger began to cry, holding a tissue to her eyes. All around the synagogue, people were watching her and Cooper talk, and Cooper felt very self-conscious as she searched for the right words to say.

"I don't know why I saw those things, either," she said finally. "But I'm glad I could help."

Mrs. Sanger took Cooper's hand and held it. Her voice was trembling as she spoke. "If you see Elizabeth again, tell her that we love her," she whispered, her voice breaking on the last word. Then she stood up and walked away, leaving Cooper to watch her go.

A moment later the rabbi came out and began the service with a prayer. He prayed in Hebrew, and although Cooper couldn't understand the words, the rabbi's voice conveyed a sense of loss and sadness that she could feel despite not knowing what exactly was being said.

"There are many aspects of my job that are not easy," the rabbi said when he had finished the prayer. "But perhaps the hardest is leading services such as this one. No matter how many times you do it, it never becomes easier. And today it is particularly difficult because of the circumstances surrounding the death of Elizabeth Sanger."

Cooper tried to listen to what the rabbbi was saying, but suddenly she didn't feel very well. Her head had begun to ache, and his words became muddy as the pain grew stronger. She rubbed her temples, trying to make the headache subside.

"Everything okay?" Annie asked her in a low voice.

Cooper nodded. The pain was lessening, and she was able to focus on the proceedings again.

"Our thoughts turn to those who have been affected by Elizabeth's death," the rabbi said. "Her family. Her friends. Those whose lives she touched. None of them will forget her."

The pain in her head returned, making her wince. What was causing it? It didn't feel like any headache she'd ever had before. The synagogue was hot. Maybe that was it. The collar of her shirt felt suddenly too tight, and she pulled at it.

He's here. The voice broke through her thoughts like a splash of icy water. And Cooper knew who was speaking them.

Elizabeth? she thought. *Is that you?*

He's here, the voice said again. It was definitely Elizabeth's voice.

No, Cooper thought. *Not again.* Was she about to have another vision? Was that why her head hurt so badly? She didn't know if she could stand to see anything else right now. Besides, she'd led them to Elizabeth's body. What more did she have to do?

He's here, the voice said for a third time. This time it seemed to come from outside her head. She looked up and saw Elizabeth standing at the front of the synagogue. She was still dressed in jeans and a sweatshirt, as she had been the other times Cooper had seen her. She stood beside the rabbi as he continued to talk, oblivious to the fact that a ghost was beside him, the ghost of the girl whose life and death were the subjects of the service.

Who's here? Cooper thought the words, knowing that she was not in a trance but sitting in the very real synagogue with very real people all around her. If she spoke, she knew they would hear her.

The man who killed me, Elizabeth answered. She

looked at Cooper, her eyes empty and dark. *I know he's here.*

Cooper wanted to stand up and look around. If Elizabeth's murderer was there, she could point him out and he could be caught. But she had no idea who she was looking for or what he looked like. And she knew that Elizabeth hadn't seen her attacker.

How do you know? she thought.

I can sense his hatred, Elizabeth responded. *It drew me here. I can taste it.*

Cooper's head felt ready to burst. She wondered suddenly if she was again experiencing what Elizabeth was experiencing, the way she had tasted the oily rag that had been shoved into Elizabeth's mouth when she was kidnapped. Maybe the pain was being caused by the hatred Elizabeth sensed coming from her killer. If it was, then his emotions were more intense than anything Cooper had ever felt before in her life.

How do I find him? she asked Elizabeth. *How do I know who he is?*

There was no answer. Cooper looked up again and saw that Elizabeth had stepped down from where the rabbi was standing. She was looking out at the congregation, searching the faces she saw there.

She's looking for him, Cooper thought to herself as she watched Elizabeth. *She's trying to sense his energy.*

Elizabeth walked slowly down the aisle that ran

between the rows of pews. When she came to her mother and father, she paused and looked at them. She reached out and touched her mother's face, and Cooper saw Mrs. Sanger put her hand to her cheek and look directly at Elizabeth.

She can't see her, Cooper thought. Yet somehow Mrs. Sanger had sensed her daughter's presence. Cooper wanted to go to her, to tell her that Elizabeth was there and that she knew her parents missed her. But she was rooted to her seat, watching the ghost of the dead girl make its way through the congregation.

Cooper became more and more tense as she watched Elizabeth search for her killer. What was she going to do when Elizabeth found him? There were no police around to help Cooper if she had to act on her own. And would anyone believe her if she accused someone of having murdered Elizabeth? Everyone thought Christopher Barrons was guilty. What would they think if it turned out to be someone else? Particularly if it was someone Elizabeth had known? After all, the people assembled in the synagogue were supposed to be people who had cared about her. Why would one of them want her dead?

The pain in Cooper's head increased. She had to clench her fingers into a fist, her nails biting into her palms, to keep from crying out. The headache was excruciating. It was as if all of Elizabeth's rage were flowing through Cooper's veins, mixing with the thoughts of her killer, and forming a deadly poison. Cooper wasn't sure she could stand it. Reaching over, she grabbed Annie's hand.

"What is it?" Annie whispered. "Are you sick?" She leaned in to hear what Cooper wanted.

"Elizabeth," Cooper said, forcing the word out. "She's here."

Annie looked around. "Where?" she said. "Do you see her?"

Cooper nodded, causing her head to throb. She wasn't sure she could speak. "Looking," she said finally, the effort making her dizzy. "For . . . her . . . killer." Forming each word took a tremendous effort, and when she was done she closed her eyes tightly, trying to will the pain away.

"He's here?" Annie said anxiously. "Do you know where?"

Cooper shook her head slowly. She needed to find Elizabeth, to see where she had gone. She knew the girl must be nearing her killer, because the pain was washing over her in waves.

Looking over her shoulder, she searched the synagogue for Elizabeth. She was nearing the last few rows. Cooper looked to see who was sitting in them. She saw Mr. Niemark, one of the math teachers from school. She saw Detective Stern, who appeared to be wearing the same clothes he'd had on the last time Cooper had seen him. She saw a man she recognized as one of her father's wealthy clients. But mostly she saw a lot of faces she didn't know. One of them was apparently Elizabeth's killer. But which one? There were too many.

Elizabeth paused. She seemed confused, as if she didn't know where to go. She put her hand to her head. As she did, Cooper felt a blinding stab of pain that made her lower her head into her hands. Annie put an arm around her shoulders.

"Cooper?" she asked, concern in her voice. "What's happening?"

It's him. Elizabeth's voice came through the pain. She sounded frightened. She had apparently found her killer, and she was sending out a steady stream of emotions: fear, anger, rage. They all bombarded Cooper like a torrent of water, forcing her head down, making it impossible for her to see the person Elizabeth was pointing an accusing finger at.

I can't see, she thought. *Your feelings are too strong.* She tried to fight the onslaught, to push against it. It was her only chance. If she could just look, she could see the man responsible for killing Elizabeth. If she could just raise her head.

"Come on, Cooper," Annie said beside her. "Whatever is happening, fight it."

Hearing her friend's encouragement, Cooper lifted her head. Every movement was pure pain, but she forced herself to do it. She looked up. Elizabeth was standing in the aisle, her hand stretched out and trembling.

It's him, she said. *He's the one.* This time, she sounded surprised as well as angry.

Cooper looked where Elizabeth's hand was pointing. There were a number of men sitting in the pew, their faces blurred behind the pain that pounded in Cooper's head. She couldn't distinguish one from the other, no matter how hard she tried to focus. She knew Elizabeth was waiting desperately for her to identify the man, to make him known. But she couldn't do it. The pain was too much for her. Giving a cry of defeat, she surrendered to it and felt herself sink into blackness.

"Cooper?"

Someone was standing over her. Her eyes fluttered open, and she saw that she was lying in the aisle of the synagogue. People were looking down at her, and all she could see was a forest of black-trousered legs and the hems of dresses.

Elizabeth. Suddenly she remembered what had happened. She had to see if Elizabeth was still there. She tried to sit up, but the pain in her head forced her back down.

"Don't move," someone said. "We'll help you up."

Several arms went around her and helped her stand. She could see that everyone had gotten up to see what was going on. "That's the girl," she heard someone say. "The one who told them where the body was."

"Are you all right?" one of the men holding her up said.

Cooper nodded. "I just need to get some air."

As they helped her to the back of the synagogue, Cooper realized that she had fainted. Even worse, she had interrupted Elizabeth's memorial service.

"I'm sorry," she kept saying as she walked slowly down the aisle. "I didn't mean to."

"It's okay," Annie said. She and Kate were beside Cooper, walking with her. "Don't talk."

When they reached the back of the synagogue, one of the men offered to call a doctor. But Annie told him that Cooper was just overheated and tired, and that they would make sure she got home. After they were satisfied that Cooper would be all right, the men left the girls alone.

"What happened back there?" Kate asked. Because she had been sitting on the other side of Annie, she hadn't witnessed any of what had occurred.

"Cooper saw Elizabeth," Annie explained. "She was trying to tell her who the killer was. Were you able to find out, Cooper?"

Cooper shook her head. "She was pointing at him, but it was too much," she said. "I couldn't handle the pain."

Now that the pain was going away, it was being replaced by anger. She'd had a chance to catch Elizabeth's killer, and she'd blown it. If only she'd been able to hold out for another few seconds. Then she had a thought.

"Did anyone leave?" she asked Annie and Kate. "When I fainted? Did anyone get up and leave?"

Kate and Annie looked at one another. "Everyone got up since the service was pretty much over," Kate said. "People were moving all over the place. Someone could have skipped out."

"But he could still be in there!" Cooper said. "We have to try again."

She tried to get up, but her knees gave out and she sat again. She knew she wouldn't be able to handle another experience like the one she'd just gone through. Besides, something told her that Elizabeth's killer was long gone.

"Another one of your mysterious episodes?"

Cooper looked up. Amanda Barclay was standing in front of her.

"Where did you come from?" Cooper asked. "Hiding underneath one of the pews?"

Amanda frowned. "Why wouldn't I be here?" she asked. "After all, it was me who discovered the link between Elizabeth Sanger and Christopher Barrons. And I didn't need any visions to do it."

"Barrons didn't—" Cooper started to say.

"Maybe you should go," Annie interrupted. "Cooper isn't feeling very well right now."

"If Cooper has something to say, I'd be glad to hear it," Amanda said. "After all, everyone would love to hear from the girl who saw a ghost."

She paused, waiting for Cooper to say something else.

"No," Cooper said flatly. "I don't have anything to say."

Amanda Barclay scowled. Then she turned and walked away, leaving the girls alone again.

"At least not to you," Cooper added, speaking to Amanda's retreating back.

CHAPTER 11

Bailey Maron pushed her hair out of her eyes, smearing a streak of blue paint across her forehead in the process. She looked irritably at the paintbrush in her hand as if it were some kind of living thing that had deliberately attacked her. Behind her, the piece of scenery she had been painting when she'd been interrupted waited to be finished, half of the sky filled in above a field of green grass.

"Sorry to bother you," Cooper said.

"No," said Bailey. "It's okay." She was a slight girl, dressed in faded overalls and a bright blue shirt. Her brown hair was all over the place, and there were little flecks of paint in various colors on her round, wire-rimmed glasses.

It was Thursday morning. Cooper, Annie, and Kate were supposed to be in various classes, but instead they were standing in the art room, where they'd tracked Bailey down. She was busy painting scenery for the upcoming school play.

"You're the girl who found Elizabeth, right?" Bailey asked.

"Sort of," said Cooper. "I just told the police where to look."

Bailey smiled, but she looked sad. "I still can't believe she's gone," she said. "She was a friend of mine. We were supposed to go to a movie the night she disappeared."

"I know," Cooper responded. "That's why I'm here. I was wondering if you could tell us anything about Elizabeth. Like maybe what she did that day."

"I told the police everything already," said Bailey. "Are you helping them some more or something?"

Cooper didn't really know what to say. She didn't want to upset Bailey by telling her that they were trying to figure out who really killed Elizabeth Sanger. She figured that, like most people, Bailey probably believed that Christopher Barrons had kidnapped and murdered her friend.

"No," she said, deciding to tell at least part of the truth. "I'm not working with the police. I'm just trying to figure some things out, is all."

"About the visions?" Bailey asked. "I read about them in the paper."

"That's part of it," Cooper said, hoping Bailey would leave it at that. "I just wondered if you could tell me anything about her life. I didn't really know her at all."

Bailey put the paintbrush she was holding into

a jar filled with murky water. "I met Elizabeth when I volunteered for Drama Club," she said. "She and I worked together on the sets for *My Fair Lady* last fall. She didn't talk much at first, but she was really funny. I guess we just became friends by default, really."

Cooper looked at Kate and Annie. They certainly knew all about becoming friends with people you never thought you would hang out with. She would never have thought to even talk to Annie or Kate before the whole incident with the spell book brought them together. Now she couldn't imagine not having them around. She knew Elizabeth's absence must be really hard for Bailey.

"Did she have any other friends?" Annie asked. "Anyone else she hung out with?"

"Rachel Huctwith," Bailey replied. "She's the other girl who was with me the night Elizabeth was kidnapped. But she doesn't go to Beecher. She goes to St. Basil's."

"That's where Tyler goes," Kate exclaimed. St. Basil's was a private Catholic school in town. Tyler, despite his and his mother's involvement in Wicca, went there because his father insisted on it.

"How did Rachel know Elizabeth, then?" Kate asked.

"Elizabeth had a job after school," explained Bailey. "She worked at this used clothing store downtown."

"And Rachel worked there too?" asked Annie.

"No," Bailey answered. "Her brother did. I think his name is Dan. Elizabeth met Rachel through him."

"And you guys were supposed to go to a movie the night Elizabeth disappeared, right?" Cooper said.

Bailey nodded. "Rachel and I met up at the theater. We waited for Elizabeth, and when she didn't show up we got worried and called her parents."

"Do you know what else she did that day?" asked Cooper.

"Her mother said she was home all day working on a paper," Bailey said. "She was going to stop by the store to do something, and then she was supposed to come to the movie."

"The store?" Annie said. "You mean the one she worked at?"

"Right," Bailey said. "Alice's Attic is the name of it. She was going to stop there and then meet us at the theater."

"Do you know if she went there?" asked Kate.

"I'm not sure," Bailey said. "To tell the truth, I haven't read much of the stuff that's been in the papers. I told the police what I know, but that's really it. Oh, and that reporter who asked me about Elizabeth. I talked to her."

"Reporter?" Cooper said. "You don't mean Amanda Barclay?"

"That's her," Bailey confirmed. "She came to

my house the other night asking all kinds of questions. She pretty much asked me the same things you did."

"Well, thanks for answering them all again," Cooper said. "I appreciate it."

Bailey smiled and pushed up her glasses. "Elizabeth was a really nice girl," she said quietly. "I know she wasn't popular or anything, but she was fun to hang out with and talk to. She would never hurt anyone. I don't know why someone would want to kill her. I guess that guy is just crazy. I'm glad you helped catch him."

"Amanda Barclay did that," Cooper said. "She's the one who made the connection between Elizabeth and Christopher Barrons."

"Anyway," Bailey said. "Thanks. It makes it a little easier knowing what happened."

Cooper nodded. Once again, she thought about how what people really wanted was answers. They wanted to know who killed Elizabeth Sanger, and why. Putting a face on the crime helped them deal with how they were feeling. Even if that face wasn't the right one, it was at least some kind of answer, some kind of explanation for what had happened.

But isn't that what you want too? she asked herself. *Aren't you looking for the same answers?* She was. But she wasn't willing to accept the easiest one, or even the one that seemed to make the most sense. She didn't believe that Christopher Barrons had murdered

Elizabeth. Even more important, Elizabeth didn't believe it, either.

But what if Elizabeth was also looking for an easy answer? Did she really know who had killed her? She'd said that she couldn't remember who the murderer was. Was it possible for the dead to be blinded by their fear and anger just like the living were? Cooper didn't know. But for now she had to trust what her instincts—and Elizabeth—told her.

They left Bailey to finish painting and walked out of the art room. Back in the hallway, they stood and talked.

"What now?" Kate asked. "Do we try to talk to this Rachel Huctwith?"

"She'll probably just tell us the same things Bailey did," Annie said. "I don't think they know anything else."

"What about the brother?" Cooper asked. "Maybe we could talk to him. At least we could find out whether or not Elizabeth ever made it to the store that night."

"What was it called?" Annie said. "Alice's Attic? Do you know where it is?"

"We can find out easily enough," Cooper answered as the bell rang for the next period. "Meet me after school."

Alice's Attic was in a part of town that could only kindly be described as run-down. Unlike the waterfront, where Crones' Circle was located, the area around the small store was filled with pawnshops, liquor stores, and places that sold cheap items to people who could ill afford even those low prices. As the girls walked down the street, more than one person asked them for spare change.

Sprinkled in between the sad-looking stores were some freshly painted buildings that provided bright spots in the midst of the bleakness, like flowers growing through the cracks of a dirty sidewalk. It was as if these new, fresh stores were trying to revitalize the area and give it some much-needed hope. Alice's Attic was located in one of these buildings. The sign outside was painted a cheerful yellow and blue, and when they went inside they were greeted by a smiling young woman with multiple rings in each ear, not to mention in her nose.

"Hi," she said. "Welcome to Alice's Attic. Are you looking for something in particular?"

"Is Dan here by any chance?" Cooper asked, hoping Bailey had gotten the guy's name right.

"Dan!" the girl shouted. "Someone wants to see you." She pointed to the back of the store. "Go on back," she said. "If he's not out in a minute, just yell again."

Cooper and the others made their way through the store. Alice's Attic was a funky clothing store, and they passed racks of dresses, shirts, and other items. A lot of the stuff looked like it was vintage, and normally Cooper would have stopped to look through everything. She was particularly interested in the store's large selection of Doc Marten boots. The ones she wore almost constantly were wearing out, and the store had some cool new styles she'd never seen before. But right then she was looking for something besides clothes.

A young man was coming out from behind a black velvet curtain when they reached the rear of the store. He was tall and muscular, with numerous tattoos on his arms. His black hair was slicked back, and a wallet on a chain was tucked into the back pocket of his black jeans. When he saw the girls, he smiled warmly.

"Can I help you guys with something?" he asked.

"Maybe," Cooper said. "We were wondering if you could tell us something about Elizabeth Sanger."

Dan looked at them closely. "You three don't look like cops," he said lightly. "Unless I'm getting *really* old."

Cooper laughed. "No cops," she said. "We went to school with Elizabeth. Bailey Maron told us you might have some information about her."

Dan shrugged. "She worked here for about the last six months," he said, sighing. "Nice kid. Worked here after school and some weekends. She hung out a lot with my little sister."

"Her mother said she was coming here the night she disappeared," Annie said. "Did she ever make it?"

"No," Dan said, shaking his head. "That's what made me suspicious that it might have been someone around here who abducted her. She was supposed to come pick up her paycheck, but she never got here. When they figured out she was missing, I started asking around to see if anyone had seen her that night. Elizabeth had a good heart, you know. She would talk to just about anyone. She was always talking to bums on the street. I told her she probably shouldn't, but she felt bad for them."

"She talked to people on the street?" Cooper asked.

"Yeah," said Dan. "You probably noticed that there are a lot of homeless types around here. She knew a lot of them by name. Frankly, I wasn't all that surprised when I heard about that Barrons guy trying to pawn her necklace."

"Had you ever seen Barrons before?" Cooper asked.

"Sure," Dan answered. "He was a drifter. Came around here every once in a while. I paid him to do odd jobs a couple of times. I never thought he would do something like this, though. Most of these guys are actually pretty decent."

"So Elizabeth knew him?" Annie said.

"The same way she knew a lot of the street

people," Dan told her. "I'm sure she said hello to him when she saw him. And she would have known him from the store."

"But why would he kill her?" Kate asked.

"Your guess is as good as mine," Dan said. "Maybe he thought she had some money on her. I don't know. A lot of these guys aren't quite right in the head. He probably just snapped."

Dan had been looking at Cooper for some time while they'd been talking. Now he pointed his finger at her and cocked his head. "You're Cooper Rivers," he said.

"Guilty," Cooper responded.

"I wondered why three high school kids would be so interested in what happened to Elizabeth," he said. "Now it makes sense. So, did you really see who killed her?"

Cooper shook her head. "That's the problem," she said. "I didn't see anything about who did it. Just where her body was."

"I don't get it," Dan said. "The police arrested Barrons. He had her necklace and her backpack. Looks pretty black-and-white to me. He knew who she was, so she would have trusted him if he came up to her on the street. My guess is that he dragged her somewhere, knocked her out, and then took her to that house."

"I know," Cooper admitted. "It all makes a lot of sense. But Elizabeth doesn't think he did it."

"Elizabeth?" Dan said. "She talked to you?"

"In the visions," Cooper said. "I didn't just see her. I talked to her. And she says that someone else killed her."

Dan looked confused. "The paper didn't say anything about that," he said.

"That's because I won't talk to them," Cooper informed him. "Especially Amanda Barclay, the one who broke the story. All she knows is whatever her source at the police station told her. But yeah, Elizabeth has talked to me. And as long as she says Barrons didn't do it, I believe her."

"Have you told anybody else about this?" Dan asked. "I mean, do the police know?"

Cooper snorted. "No one would believe me anyway," she answered. "They already think I'm wired wrong because I saw what I saw."

"You have to admit, it is pretty weird," he said. "Talking to a dead girl? I know it's all the rage in the movies and all that, but you don't exactly hear about it every day. And I doubt it would stand up at a trial."

"All I know is what I see," Cooper said. "Maybe Barrons really did kill Elizabeth. I just wish we had more proof."

"Well, I've got all the proof I need," Dan said. "I feel sorry for the guy, but I feel worse for Elizabeth. She was a good kid. Everyone will really miss her around here. We were all relieved when they found her, thanks to your visions or whatever.

You should feel good about that."

"Thanks," said Cooper. "I do."

Back outside, Cooper looked up and down the sidewalks at the street people leaning against cars and walls, talking to one another and sometimes to themselves.

"What are you thinking?" Kate asked her. "I know that look. You're upset about something."

"I was thinking about Christopher Barrons," Cooper said.

"What about him?" asked Annie.

"Do you think he's guilty?"

"I don't know," Annie answered. "The evidence looks pretty strong against him."

"I know Elizabeth doesn't think he did it," Kate added. "But she also said she couldn't really remember. Do you think ghosts can get confused?"

"I want to ask Robin about that," Cooper said. "But something else occurred to me while Dan was talking."

Kate and Annie waited for her to continue.

"He was supposedly homeless, right?" said Cooper.

Her friends nodded. "I think the politically correct term is drifter," Annie said.

Cooper looked at them. "How many homeless people do you know with cars?" she asked.

Annie looked confused. "What do you mean?"

"No one could have carried Elizabeth to that

house," Cooper said. "It's too far. Besides, in my first dream I was definitely locked in a car trunk. So that makes me wonder—where did Christopher Barrons get a car?"

CHAPTER 12

Cooper looked at the list she'd just finished writing in her notebook. One by one she read off the names. "Christopher Barrons. Arthur Perch. Elizabeth Sanger. John and Rebecca Sanger. Bailey Maron. Rachel Huctwith."

She looked at the people gathered around her. She was sitting on the bed in Annie's attic bedroom. Kate, Annie, Sasha, and Tyler were seated on cushions on the floor. It was Friday afternoon, after school, and they had met to talk about what was going on. Cooper thought the more heads they had working on the problem, the quicker they might be able to work it out.

"These are all the people who are connected in some way with Elizabeth's death," she said. "Barrons, of course, is the one everybody thinks did it. Arthur Perch is the guy whose house they found her in. The other four are the last people who probably saw Elizabeth alive. And actually, Rachel Huctwith didn't even see her that day. But she *was* Elizabeth's friend. Tyler, what do you know about her? You go to school with her."

"Not a lot," he said. "She's a freshman. She sings in the choir. That's about it, I think."

"I don't suppose she has a car?" Cooper said.

"Not that I know of. Plus, she's too young to drive," Tyler said. "Why?"

Cooper explained what had been bothering her about Christopher Barrons—how he couldn't have taken Elizabeth to the house by Lake Dryer without a car.

"Maybe he stole one," Sasha suggested. "It's not that hard."

They all turned and looked at her.

"I didn't say I've ever *done* it," she said. "Sheesh. You run away and suddenly everybody thinks you know how to forge checks and make explosives out of tampons and hand lotion."

"But why would he?" said Cooper. "Why would he even bother taking her way out there? If all he wanted was money, he could have just snatched her backpack and run off with it. Whoever kidnapped Elizabeth knew what he was doing."

"What about this Perch guy?" Kate said. "It was his house, after all."

"I took advantage of our education system and used the library computer to look him up today," Annie said. She opened her backpack and took out a couple of pieces of paper. "These are all the newspaper reports about his wife's death. Remember, the articles in the *Tribune* said that's why he didn't use the house by the lake anymore."

"What happened to her?" asked Cooper.

"She fell down the stairs," said Annie. "Broke her neck. Nothing too exciting, as far as dramatic deaths go."

"Not unless someone pushed her," said Kate.

"That's cheery," Tyler said. "Are you saying I should be careful the next time we're near steps?"

"I'm just thinking out loud," said Kate. "Since we're on the subject of murder and all, it just crossed my mind." She'd also been thinking of the time she and Annie had been accused of pushing someone down some steps. In that instance, it had also been an accident.

"The articles don't say anything about any suspicion of foul play," Annie said.

"Anyway, Perch was out of town the night of Elizabeth's murder," Kate reminded them.

"There is something interesting about the articles, though," Annie said. "Guess who wrote one of them?"

"Let me guess," said Cooper. "Our friend Amanda?"

"That's the one," said Annie. "It wasn't for any of the big papers, just a small one. It was probably one of the first things she ever wrote."

"Arthur Perch is probably lucky she didn't finger him at the time," Cooper mused. "He'd probably be in jail for murdering his wife."

"So we've eliminated Perch," Tyler said. "And I assume we've eliminated Rachel Huctwith and Bailey Maron, right?"

"Right," said Cooper. "Too small to carry the body."

"What about the parents?" Kate said. "We still have them."

"Too movie-of-the-week," Annie said. "I know it makes a good story, but that's something Amanda Barclay would dream up."

"Annie's right," said Cooper. "Her parents didn't do it. We saw them at the memorial service, and they were a wreck."

"Then that leaves Christopher Barrons," Sasha said. "We're back to square one."

"It's true," Kate said. "No one else saw Elizabeth that night. No one else was found with her stuff."

"Why can't you just ask Elizabeth who she saw in the synagogue?" Sasha asked. "Or is that a dumb question?"

"No," Cooper said. "It's not a dumb question. The problem is, I've tried asking Elizabeth. I can't get her to come to me. I keep hoping she'll show up in a dream, but she doesn't."

"Do you know why?" Sasha said.

"I talked to Robin last night," Cooper answered. "She told me that sometimes when a person has had a very strong psychic experience the mind will refuse to allow anything else in for a while. It's like when you overdo it playing soccer and you have to let your leg muscles rest up. What happened at Elizabeth's memorial service really did a number on me, so Robin thinks my brain is just on strike while it gets over it."

"What about having someone else try to contact her?" Annie suggested.

Cooper shook her head. "I thought of that. According to Robin, the dead usually pick one person to contact. They form a connection, and it's hard for them to just switch over to someone else."

"So Elizabeth could be trying to get through but can't?" said Kate.

"Right," Cooper said. "At least not until I'm ready for her to come back."

She hated admitting that she might be the one responsible for leaving the mystery of Elizabeth's death unsolved. There she was, trying to get everyone to help her figure out what had happened, and the answer was right there in her head, if only she could allow Elizabeth to come through again. If she hadn't reacted so strongly the last time Elizabeth had appeared, this would probably all be over now. But it wasn't, and she didn't know when she would be recovered enough to talk to Elizabeth again.

"I guess that's all we can do for right now," she said. "We've pretty much run out of ideas. And I have to get home anyway."

Her father had been able to run interference with her mother over the issue of Cooper's attending the Wicca study group, but her mom was still angry about what had happened and had insisted that Cooper be home early whenever possible. Tonight she'd declared her curfew to be six o'clock. Cooper thought her mother was being ridiculous, but she didn't want to do anything that would make her do something even more extreme—like tell Cooper she couldn't go to Crones' Circle anymore.

As she walked home, she thought how much more fun it would be to be riding in the Nash. She had barely even had an opportunity to sit in her new car since she'd gotten it, let alone drive it anywhere. *Maybe this weekend*, she thought. It would be nice to get out on the road, away from all the tension at home and school.

But right now she had her mother to deal with. As she walked up her street, she wondered what kind of mood her mom would be in when she got home. For the most part, the two of them had maintained a frosty silence ever since Cooper's remark about her grandmother. It bothered Cooper a lot, because normally she and her mother got along reasonably well. But she didn't know how to bring up the subject without getting into a huge discussion—or, worse, a fight about it.

"Penny for your thoughts," a voice said.

She turned and saw Amanda Barclay driving slowly alongside her. The window of her blue Volkswagen Jetta was rolled down, and she was leaning out. Cooper groaned.

"What do you want?" she asked the reporter.

"Just to talk," Amanda said. "I have a proposition."

Cooper stopped, and Amanda brought the car to a halt.

"Why would I want to talk to you?" Cooper said. "You've basically made me the town freak."

"I don't think anyone thinks you're a freak," Amanda said.

Cooper arched an eyebrow. "Oh, yeah? Want to listen to the messages on my answering machine?"

"Oh, those," said Amanda, waving her hand dismissively. "You can't listen to those. I get those all the time."

"Gee, I can't imagine why," Cooper said as sarcastically as possible. "Did you ever think that maybe it's because you print people's names when they don't want them printed? And how did you find out about me, anyway? Was it Stern? Did he tell you?"

Amanda opened the car door and got out, coming to stand in front of Cooper. She was dressed in a neat blue suit that matched her car, and she was carrying her ever-present notebook.

"I never reveal my sources," she said. "But just for your information, no, I did not find out about you from Stern. He wouldn't even talk to me. I read it in his report."

"And how did you get *that*?" Cooper demanded. She couldn't believe Amanda had managed to get her hands on what was supposed to be privileged information.

"That has to remain my little secret," Amanda said. "A girl can't give away everything. But let's just say you can get just about anything if you know the right people."

"So what do you want from me?" Cooper said. "You told me you had a proposition. What is it?"

"An exchange of information," Amanda said. "I hear through the grapevine that you don't think Barrons killed Elizabeth Sanger."

"And who told you that?" asked Cooper. "Wait, let me guess, a confidential source?"

Amanda Barclay smiled. "You're catching on," she said. "So, why don't you think he did it?"

"Why should I tell you anything?" said Cooper. "So you can write another article? I don't think so."

Amanda opened her notebook. "I'm going to write one anyway," she said. "You might as well be quoted accurately."

Cooper knew that Amanda meant what she said. If she didn't talk, the reporter would just write whatever she wanted to, including just enough of the truth that no one could accuse her of making it all up. Cooper's father had been right—Amanda *was* smart. Just not in the way he thought she was.

"You said an exchange of information," Cooper said. "What do I get out of this?"

"A sneak peek at the story I'm working on," Amanda said. "I've uncovered more evidence against Barrons."

"What kind of evidence?" Cooper asked. She

would never admit it to Amanda Barclay, but she was curious.

"You first," the writer responded. "What makes you think Barrons *didn't* do it?"

Cooper weighed the pros and cons of talking to Amanda Barclay. Whatever she said was going to end up in print. That meant that people would be talking about her again. And if she implied that the police had arrested the wrong man, she knew that would make a lot of people angry. But apparently Amanda had uncovered some more information. She claimed it implicated Barrons. But maybe it would give Cooper the break she needed to move forward.

"Okay," Cooper said. "I'll talk to you. But just for a minute—and you'd better not misquote me."

"I'm taking down every word," Amanda said, her pen at the ready.

Cooper told her, in general terms, how Elizabeth's spirit had told her that Barrons wasn't the killer. She was as vague as possible, leaving out details and giving Amanda the bare bones version of what she'd experienced.

"So that's what happened at the memorial service," Amanda said. "You fainted because you saw Elizabeth's ghost."

"No," Cooper said. "I fainted because I was exhausted and had a wicked headache." She wasn't about to tell the nosy reporter that Elizabeth had been about to unmask her murderer and that

Cooper hadn't been able to handle it.

Amanda looked at her quizzically but didn't press her. She seemed satisfied with what she had. She closed her notebook and put away the pen.

"Now it's your turn," Cooper said. "What is it you've found out."

"Elizabeth Sanger isn't the first girl Christopher Barrons killed," Amanda said. She smiled triumphantly at Cooper, as if she'd just won some kind of contest.

"What do you mean?" Cooper said. "He murdered someone else?"

"Well, they didn't call it murder," Amanda said. "But he killed her all the same. Seven years ago Christopher Barrons was a successful computer programmer with a drinking problem. One night he went out with his buddies, had a little too much to drink, and tried to drive home. On the way, he hit and killed a fifteen-year-old girl. He spent a couple of years in prison for it. When he got out, no one would hire him. That's when he became homeless. He's been moving from city to city ever since."

"Just because he killed someone accidentally doesn't mean he killed Elizabeth," Cooper said. "You're just assuming that he would do something like that."

Amanda Barclay pulled something from her pocket and held it in front of Cooper. It was a picture of a girl.

"That looks like Elizabeth," Cooper said.

"I know," Amanda replied. "But it isn't. It's Kim Fisher. The other girl Barrons killed. Kind of creepy, isn't it?"

"You think because they look alike he must have killed Elizabeth?" Cooper said, astonished.

Amanda put the photo back into her pocket. "I think because Elizabeth Sanger looked like Kim Fisher, Barrons was attracted to her. It turns out that he spoke to her often."

"She talked to a lot of the street people," Cooper countered.

"But Barrons tried to get Elizabeth to go places with him," the journalist continued. "People often saw him begging her to come with him. I think he got the two girls mixed up in his poor, confused mind and ended up taking out his guilt about Kim on Elizabeth."

"Who told you all of this?" Cooper asked.

"Sources," said Amanda primly. "Reliable ones."

"And you're telling me this because you want me to change my mind, is that it?" said Cooper.

Amanda shook her head. "Frankly, it makes a better story if you keep saying Barrons is innocent," she said. "But you're just going to look foolish if you do. I'm trying to save you the trouble."

Cooper didn't know whether to believe what she was hearing or not. Amanda Barclay had never shown any interest in helping her before. Why should she do it now? But she *had* told Cooper practically her entire scoop, and Cooper knew that was a big risk.

"Well, that's all I wanted to say," Amanda said. "I guess I'll be going now."

She turned to get back into her car. As she did, a piece of paper slipped out of her notebook and fluttered to the ground. Cooper bent down and picked it up. She was about to call after Amanda, but the reporter had already gotten into her car and was pulling away.

Cooper unfolded the paper. There was a telephone number written on it. Next to the numbers was written, "Call regarding Sanger murder/Barrons connection. 10:45 P.M. Thursday, 05/05."

Cooper stared at the number. Amanda Barclay had called someone at that number the night before. Probably the person who gave her all of the information she had just shared with Cooper. But who did the number belong to? It could have been anyone's. As soon as Cooper got home, she was going to find out.

CHAPTER 13

Before Cooper could find out who the phone number belonged to, though, she had to deal with her mother.

When she entered the house, Cooper discovered her mother in the kitchen, trying to cook dinner. Several pots boiled on the stove, their contents sending out mysterious clouds of odd-smelling steam. Her mother had the oven door open and was peering inside with an anxious expression.

"What's all this?" Cooper asked.

Her mother poked whatever was in the oven with a long fork, frowned, and shut the door. "I thought it would be nice if we had a normal family dinner," her mother said.

"And how's it going?" Cooper asked.

"Badly," said her mother. "And you're late."

"Just a few minutes," Cooper answered. She knew she couldn't tell her mother that she was late because she'd stopped to talk to Amanda Barclay. She would be furious.

"Cooper," her mother said, "I'm doing the best I can to make things normal around here. I wish you would try to help."

"Things *are* normal," said Cooper. "You don't have to do anything like . . . this." She waved at the stove, which was smoking, and at the pots, which were boiling over. Her mother frantically tried to turn off the burners and close the oven door at the same time.

"It is not normal to be seeing dead girls," her mother said. "Or to be taking witchcraft lessons."

Cooper reddened. "They aren't lessons," she said. "It's a class for learning about Wicca. For your information, it happens to be a religion, not some kind of hobby."

"Don't lecture me, young lady," her mother snapped. "Your father might not think there's anything wrong with what you're doing, but he doesn't know how dangerous it is."

"It's not dangerous," Cooper insisted. "It's all about nature and connecting with the world. It's not about doing anything that could hurt anyone."

"It's not normal," her mother said. She was standing with her arms folded, looking at Cooper with an expression Cooper had never seen on her face—a mixture of fear and hurt. "I'm sorry if hearing that makes you unhappy, but it's how I feel. You didn't grow up with a mother people thought was crazy. You didn't hear them call her names when they walked by the house, or have them throw stones at you because they said you must be a witch."

"Did people do those things to you?" Cooper asked. Her mother had never mentioned any of this before.

Mrs. Rivers nodded. "They used to call our house the witch house," she said. "The other kids told their little brothers and sisters that my mother would throw them into the oven if they came into our yard."

"But why?" asked Cooper.

"Because she looked different," her mother answered. "Because she told fortunes for the women in the neighborhood. Because she gave them herbs to make their babies stop coughing, and made charms for girls who were getting married. Because she wasn't normal."

"That's why you got so mad when she tried to teach me things, isn't it?" Cooper said.

Her mother looked away. "She told me she had stopped," she said. "I begged her to give it up when I was about your age. I'd had enough of the teasing. I wanted my friends to come over to the house. I wanted boys to like me instead of thinking of me as the girl who lived in the witch house. I would never let her teach me any of the things she did. I didn't want to know about them."

"And she gave it all up because you asked her to?" Cooper asked. She had always wondered why her mother was so angry about the little rhymes and games her grandmother had taught her when she was little. Now it was beginning to make sense.

"Yes," she said. "She tried to act like everyone else's mother. And it worked. But I think it made her unhappy. When you were born, I told her I didn't want her trying to teach you anything. I wanted you to grow up in a totally normal way. When I found out she had broken her promise to me, I was very angry."

"And that's why you didn't talk to her for those last few years," Cooper said, finishing the story.

"I know you think I was cruel," her mother said. "But you have to understand—I didn't want you to go through what I went through. I didn't want you to feel like some kind of monster. Then, when all of this happened, I felt as if everything I'd tried to prevent had happened anyway."

"Is that what you think I am?" Cooper asked. "A monster?"

Her mother came over and put her arms around her, pulling her close. "No," she said. "I don't think you're a monster. But I do think you've chosen to do something that could be very difficult. You've already seen how people can respond when they think you're different from them."

"Do you think Grandma was really a witch?" said Cooper as her mother let go.

"She always called what she did her 'workings,'" her mother answered. "I don't know that she actually had a word for what she was."

"And do you think you inherited any of her powers?" Cooper asked hesitantly.

Her mother's face darkened. "I never tried," she said. "If I did have any of her abilities, I didn't want to know about it."

"Not even once?" Cooper said.

Her mother hesitated. "Once, when I was about twelve, I tried to put a curse on a boy at school who had been teasing me for a long time. I don't even know how I thought to do it. I just did."

"And did it work?" Cooper asked, interested.

"He fell down and broke his arm the next day," her mother said. "I was so happy. But then, a week later, I fell out of a tree I was climbing and broke *my* arm. I had to have it in a cast for most of the summer, and I was miserable. I never tried anything like that ever again."

Cooper couldn't help but think about the Law of Three, the principle of witchcraft that said if someone tried to use magic to hurt another person, the energy of that action would come back at its originator three times as strong. She wondered if her mother had any idea that she might have been the victim of her own magic, the same way Kate had been when she'd tried to do a love spell and ended up fending off practically every boy in school.

"I can't promise you that I'm going to stop what I'm doing," Cooper said. "In fact, I can pretty much guarantee that I'm not. I really like studying Wicca."

Her mother sighed. "You're as stubborn as I was

at your age," she said. "I can't say that I'm happy about your decision. But your father says those people you're learning from are okay in his book, so I guess I'm outvoted. Just promise me that you'll be careful?"

"I will," Cooper said. "And will you promise me something?"

"What?" her mother asked.

"That you'll stick to ordering dinner, and not try to make it."

"*That* I'm sure I can do," her mother answered. "Go on and get cleaned up. I'll have pizza here in half an hour."

Cooper went up to her bedroom and shut the door. She was glad that she and her mother had talked, even if all they'd managed to do was come to an uneasy truce for the moment. But now she was more curious than ever about her grandmother. Had she really been a witch? If so, where had she learned the things she knew? She'd always told Cooper that everyone where she came from could do the things she did. Was it because she wanted Cooper to think she was normal, just like everyone else? She wished her grandmother were still alive, so they could talk about these things. Maybe then she'd have a better idea of what to do to help Elizabeth.

She fished the phone number out of her pocket and looked at it. Who did it belong to? "There's one way to find out," she said, picking up the phone and dialing.

The phone rang. As she waited for someone to answer, Cooper realized that she had no idea what she was going to say. She'd just dialed without really thinking about it. What if the person was angry? What if it was someone who could trace where the call was coming from? Once again, she thought, she'd done something impulsive without thinking about what the consequences might be.

The phone was still ringing. Cooper was about to hang up when someone finally answered.

"Hello?" said a man's voice. He sounded tired, as if he'd just been woken up. In the background, Cooper could hear what sounded like a fight.

"Hello," Cooper said, unsure of what to say next. "Can you tell me where I'm calling, please?"

The man grunted. "You don't know where you're calling," he said. "What kind of crazy are you, lady?"

Cooper couldn't imagine the person she was talking to. He was laughing, and she heard him talking to someone who was apparently in the same room. "This girl is on the phone, and she don't know where she's calling."

Cooper heard more laughter. Then the man came on the line again. "You must have a wrong number," he said. "This here's a pay phone."

"Pay phone?" Cooper said. "Where?"

"Corner of Boylston and Chestnut," the man said. "Right outside of the Happy Hour. Why don't you come on down and join us for a drink? Sounds like you need one."

Cooper hung up. The number belonged to a pay phone. Why would Amanda Barclay be calling someone on a pay phone? To get information. Cooper knew that. But why would anyone who knew anything about Elizabeth Sanger's murder need to use a pay phone? Cooper had been hoping that discovering where the number led would make things more clear. But this just made the mystery even more complicated.

Her mother called her down to dinner. Trying to push all thoughts about Elizabeth and the murder out of her mind, Cooper went down to eat. She wanted to at least try to make things feel normal for her mother, even if they were totally not normal in any way. For the next hour she and her parents talked about everything except witchcraft, visions, Amanda Barclay, and Elizabeth Sanger.

Afterward, Cooper went back up to her room. Everything, particularly her desk, was a mess. She had ignored her schoolwork for a while because of everything that was going on, and there were books and papers everywhere. She decided she would try to make everything in her life as normal as possible by at least catching up on some assignments.

I'm probably the only one in the entire school doing homework on a Friday night, she thought as she straightened up some of the clutter. *If this is what being different gets me, maybe my mother is right.* Picking up a pile of paper, she discovered the tape T.J. had given her on Tuesday. She hadn't even had a chance to listen to it and tell him what she thought. Deciding that schoolwork could wait a couple of minutes more, she popped the tape into her Walkman and turned it on.

She listened to the music her bandmates had recorded for her. T.J. had been right—the melody line was a little off in the guitar part. But she could fix that, and everything else was great. She especially liked the way they'd worked out the bridge between the second verse and the chorus.

She rewound the tape and grabbed the notebook in which she wrote her lyrics, opening it to the page where she'd written the song the music went to. As she listened to the song again, she sang along softly, checking out how the words sounded against the music.

"All these secrets. All these lies. Built around my heart," she sang at the chorus. "One by one, they come undone. And all that's left is truth."

Truth. The word jumped out at her. It was the word Kate had chosen during their dedication ceremony the month before, at which they'd pledged themselves to studying Wicca. They'd drawn the words out of a bowl, and they'd been told that the words they picked represented each person's particular challenge for the year and a day of study.

Cooper's word had been *connection*. At the time she hadn't really understood how that might be her challenge, but she was beginning to understand it more and more. She had been connecting to a lot of things ever since she'd decided to study witchcraft: to her friends, to her music, to a community of other people interested in Wicca. And all of the connections she was making were helping her learn a lot about herself.

Even her visions of Elizabeth could be considered a connection of a sort. Cooper still didn't really understand how or why the visions had begun, but they had definitely changed her life and presented her with new challenges. At the dedication ritual they'd been told that facing their challenges during the year was not always going to be easy. *They weren't kidding,* Cooper thought.

This particular challenge had been all about finding the truth. But how was it about connection, besides the obvious connection to Elizabeth? Cooper wondered if there was something else she was overlooking—something that related to her challenge. What were the connections in the story of Elizabeth Sanger? Everything she tried to follow ended up being a dead end, just like the telephone number that turned out to be a pay phone that anyone could have used. There had to be something she wasn't seeing, some connection between people, or places, or events that would tie everything together.

If I could just get Elizabeth to come through again, she thought, frustrated. But how? She hadn't appeared to Cooper since the memorial service in the synagogue. What had triggered her appearances the other times Cooper wasn't asleep? The birthday cake candles. The Beltane bonfire.

The visit to the house by the lake, Cooper thought suddenly. Elizabeth hadn't exactly appeared there, but Cooper had experienced the things Elizabeth had experienced while being taken there. What if she went back again? Would it bring back other memories or make something happen? After all, it was the place where Elizabeth had died. It probably contained her strongest memories. Maybe, if Cooper put herself in the same place, it would be enough to bring Elizabeth back so Cooper could find out who her killer was.

Good thing tomorrow is Saturday, she thought as she picked up the phone to call Kate and Annie.

CHAPTER 14

The Happy Hour was anything but. A dirty, rundown bar, its windows were streaked with grime, and the smells of cigarettes and beer oozed from the open doorway. Even the blinking neon sign seemed to be under the influence of the bar's liquid attractions, flashing at irregular intervals in a tired, drunken way. It was only seven o'clock, early for a Saturday night, but already there was a steady stream of patrons going in and out of the bar. A few of them stopped to stare at the three young women gathered around the pay phone that stood in front of the establishment.

"You're sure this is the number Amanda Barclay was calling?" Kate asked Cooper as they stood on the corner.

Cooper took the piece of paper that Amanda had dropped and looked at it again. She checked the numbers against those printed on the filthy paper label stuck beneath the pay phone's receiver.

"This is it, all right," she said.

"Why would someone have her call a pay phone?" Kate wondered out loud.

"That part actually makes sense," said Annie. "Think about it. If you didn't want someone to know who you were or where you were calling from, wouldn't you call them from a public phone? Even if the person you're calling has caller ID, a pay phone number isn't going to do any good."

"True," agreed Cooper. "But why *this* pay phone?"

"Because even if the police traced it, no one would want to come near it?" Kate suggested, looking around.

"Maybe," said Cooper. "But it seems awfully coincidental that someone would call Amanda Barclay from a pay phone so close to where Elizabeth was supposed to be on the night she disappeared."

"Unless whoever it is saw something," said Annie. "Maybe it was one of these homeless guys."

Cooper looked around, thinking. The corner they were standing on was right in the middle of the neighborhood where Elizabeth worked. Alice's Attic was a few blocks away. Elizabeth would probably have walked by the Happy Hour frequently. It would make sense that someone who spent a lot of time in there might have seen her or might know something about what happened to her.

"I'm going in there," Cooper said, nodding toward the door of the bar. "Maybe whoever was calling Amanda, or at least someone who knows something, is in there."

"What?" said Annie and Kate in unison.

"It will only take a minute," Cooper said.

"You can't go in there," Kate said adamantly. "That place is a pit."

"Kate's right," agreed Annie. "You can't go in there."

"Just watch me," said Cooper.

She walked to the door and started to go inside. But as she stepped through, a large man blocked her path.

"Where do you think you're going?" he asked.

Cooper looked up at the man's unsmiling face. "I'm just looking for some friends," she said.

The man snorted. "Not in here, you're not. I don't think anyone you'd be looking for is in this place, little girl. And if they are, then you probably shouldn't be friends with them. Now, get out of here."

"But—" Cooper began.

"Out," the man said again, and Cooper knew he meant business. She turned and walked back to her friends.

"Hey there," a man's voice said.

Cooper turned, ready to tell the guy off. She was embarrassed about being thrown out of the bar and being called a little girl, and she was in no mood to be messed with. But when she saw who was talking to her, she relaxed. It was Dan, the manager of Alice's Attic. He smiled and walked over to Cooper and her friends.

"What are you guys doing here?" he asked. "This isn't exactly the hot spot for the teens of Beecher Falls, unless things have really changed from when I was your age."

Cooper laughed. "No," she said. "We're just looking for someone."

Dan raised one eyebrow. "Sounds interesting," he said. "Anyone I know?"

"We don't even know him," Annie said.

Dan gave her a confused look.

"We're looking for someone who might know something about what happened to Elizabeth," Cooper explained.

"You think someone might know more about what happened to her?" said Dan. He sounded surprised.

Cooper took the piece of paper out of her pocket and showed it to him. "I found this," she told him. "The number is for this pay phone."

Dan took the paper and looked at it for a minute before handing it back to Cooper. "You found that?" he asked. "Where?"

"I didn't exactly find it," said Cooper. "Amanda Barclay dropped it and I picked it up."

"Barclay?" Dan said. "That reporter for the paper? The one who's been writing about Elizabeth?"

"That's her," Cooper answered. "Apparently, someone who knows something about what happened to Elizabeth has been calling her and feeding her information."

"But you don't know who it is?" Dan asked.

"No," said Cooper. "All we know is that the calls—or at least one of them—came from this phone."

"Did Barclay tell the cops about this?" asked Dan.

"I don't know," Cooper said. "But I doubt it. I think this is how she's been getting all of her supposed inside information. She wouldn't want to lose her scoop by telling the police anything."

"And she doesn't know that you know about it?" Dan continued.

"We haven't told anyone," Cooper responded. "Well, except you. Do you have any idea who might be calling her from here, or who might want to give her information?"

Dan shook his head. "As far as I know, she talked to just about everybody even remotely connected with Elizabeth," he said. "I don't know why someone would want to give her information anonymously."

"We thought maybe someone who goes to the Happy Hour might have seen something," Annie said.

Dan looked thoughtful. "It could be," he said. "A lot of these guys hang out here all day and all night. One of them might have seen something. Tell you what, I'll ask around. This is no place for you guys to be. Even if you could get in there, they wouldn't talk to you. But I know a lot of these guys. I'll see what I can find out. If anyone knows anything, I'll give you a call, okay?"

"That sounds good to me," Cooper answered. "But maybe I should call you. My parents are still a little freaked out about all of this. If I start getting calls from guys they don't know, it might send them over the edge."

"You can call my house," Annie suggested. "My aunt won't mind."

She wrote her number on a piece of paper and handed it to Dan, who stuck it in his pocket.

"I can't believe you guys have found out so much," he said. "Do you still think that guy they arrested didn't do it?"

Cooper sighed. "No," she said. "I don't think he did it. But unless we can prove it, he's probably going to be convicted. That's why we're trying so hard to get some kind of a lead."

Dan smiled. "Elizabeth would do the same thing," he said. "And if I can help out at all, I'll do it."

"Thanks," Cooper said. "We appreciate it."

"Now, can we get out of here?" Kate asked.

Cooper rolled her eyes at Dan, who laughed. They said good-bye to him and walked back to where Cooper had parked her car. As they drove past Dan, he waved.

"I really hope he finds something," Cooper said. "It's like everything we try turns out to be a dead end."

"Are you still determined to go back to the house?" Kate asked.

"I think I should," Cooper answered. "I think it's my best chance of triggering a vision."

Kate sighed. "This Nancy Drew stuff is a lot harder than it sounds in the books."

"Yes," Cooper said. "But we have a much cooler car than she ever did."

"Easy for you to say," Kate responded. "You're not sitting in the middle. I thought it was my turn to get the window."

They drove out of town and headed for the lake. When they were almost there, it began to rain. Cooper pulled over and put up the Nash's top. As they continued on their way, the rain pattered on the soft roof.

"I feel like I'm in a tent," Kate complained.

"This car is a classic," Cooper said defensively, turning on the wipers, which swished across the windshield in short, even strokes. The headlights cast beams of light ahead of them as they turned off the main road and onto the dirt one that ran around the lake.

"Are you sure this is the right way?" Kate asked as they bounced over the rough road.

"Yes, I'm sure," Cooper answered. "I'm the one who's been here before, remember?"

"Just checking," said Kate.

They drove for another half hour, turning onto narrower and narrower roads. For several minutes Cooper thought maybe she *didn't* know where she was going after all. She half hoped that the oily taste would return to her mouth, so that she would at least know that she was on the right track. But nothing happened except that the rain began to fall harder and the road became muddier.

Then, just as she was about to admit that she really had gotten them lost, Cooper recognized the fork in the road she had seen when she'd been driven to the house by Detective Stern. She turned the Nash down the right-hand road and kept going.

"It's up here," she said.

As they approached the house, Cooper began to feel frightened. For the first time, she realized that they were out in the middle of nowhere by themselves. She'd told her parents she was just going to drive Annie and Kate around to show off her new car. They had no idea where she really was. What if something happened to them? No one would even know to look for them there. *But what's going to happen?* Cooper thought, trying to reassure herself. They were just going to take a look around. A quick peek inside the house and they'd be gone again.

But what if you do have a vision? a voice in her head said. Cooper thought about it. She'd driven out to the house hoping to see something, But what if she did, and she reacted the way she had in the synagogue? What if they needed help?

She pushed these thoughts aside as she concentrated on navigating the Nash through the potholes that were being made worse by the rain. Several times the tires spun as she drove through muddy spots, but each time they made it through and kept going. Finally, she saw the house appearing out of the darkness.

"That's it," she said. "Perch Manor."

"How fitting for a lake house," Annie commented. "I hope we catch something."

"It's not fish we're after," Kate said as Cooper parked the car and they got out. "It's a ghost."

Cooper had remembered to bring a flashlight, and she turned it on as they walked to the house. There were strands of yellow police tape across the porch, like giant cobwebs, but the girls ducked beneath the tape and walked to the door.

"I just know we're going to get into trouble for this," Kate said. "I just know it."

Cooper ignored her, pushing against the door. To her surprise, it wasn't locked, and they were able to get inside without any trouble.

"You'd think they'd lock it," Annie said as they stepped into the hallway.

"It wasn't locked the first time I was here, either," Cooper said, remembering that Detective Stern had simply pushed the door open.

"Maybe the lock is broken," Kate suggested.

Cooper looked at the door. She turned the lock from the inside, and it moved smoothly and easily. "No," she said. "It's fine."

Looking back into the hall, she shined the flashlight around. The footsteps leading to the stairs were still there, although additional footsteps appeared around the main ones, from where the police had walked through the house. The older prints were dustier, though, and it was easy to distinguish them from the others. Cooper sighed.

"Are you okay?" Annie asked.

"So far," Cooper said. "Let's go upstairs. If anything is going to happen, it will probably happen there."

Annie and Kate followed Cooper as she walked up the stairs to the landing. At the top of the stairs, she paused.

"This is where she first tried to materialize," Cooper explained.

She closed her eyes, willing Elizabeth to speak to her or to appear. But nothing happened. All she heard was the rain on the roof—and the sounds of Annie's and Kate's anxious breathing around her.

They continued down the hallway. As they approached the door at the end of the hall, Cooper felt her pulse quicken. She knew that was where Elizabeth had been killed. She recalled the sounds she'd heard coming from the room during her nightmare—the muffled screams and the thumps. Had those been the sounds of Elizabeth dying? It made her sad to think about it.

She stopped. The door to the room was crisscrossed with police tape, just as the porch had been.

"Is that where it happened?" Annie asked.

Cooper nodded.

"Are you going in?" asked Kate.

"I think I should," Cooper said. "But you guys wait here."

"No problem," Kate said instantly.

Cooper turned the knob and pushed. The door didn't move.

"It's locked," she said, trying the knob again.

"That's weird," Annie said. "They locked this door, but they didn't lock the downstairs door?"

"There's probably evidence in there," Kate said. "Can we go now?"

Cooper sighed. "I guess there's no reason to stay," she said. "I'm not getting anything at all."

They turned and walked back to the stairs, careful to avoid the roped-off footprints of the suspected murderer. As they did, Cooper looked down at the footprints in the dust. She knew that they had been made by Elizabeth's killer. She stared at the prints, wondering what the man who had made them looked like.

As she looked more closely at the footprints, something stirred in her mind. She stopped and bent down, shining the flashlight on one of the prints.

"What's the matter?" Annie asked.

"I'm not sure," Cooper said. "There's something weird about these."

Kate and Annie knelt down and looked at the prints with Kate.

"They just look like big feet to me," Kate said.

Cooper shook her head. "Look at the shape of

the tread," she said. "Those lines. I've seen those before somewhere."

"Work boots, maybe?" Annie suggested.

"I don't think so," Cooper answered. "I just can't think of why they look familiar."

There was a sudden crack of lightning outside the house, followed by a roll of thunder. The rain began to pound on the roof.

"We should really go," Kate said. "If that road washes out any more, we'll be stuck here. And I don't know about you guys, but I'm not real excited about spending the night in this place."

Cooper wanted to look at the footprints in the dust some more, but she knew Kate was right. Reluctantly, she stood up and led her friends back down the stairs and out of the house.

"I hope we can get down the road," Annie said as they got into the car and Cooper started it up.

"Don't worry," she answered. "This car will be fine."

She pulled onto the dirt road and began the long drive back to the main road. The rain had made things slippery, but she was careful to maneuver the car around the biggest potholes, and they were soon on the larger road that led to the highway.

"I really wish I could have gotten through to Elizabeth tonight," Cooper said.

Annie patted her arm. "Maybe you just need more rest," she said. "Robin said those visions you had really wore you out. It will just take time."

"But we don't have time!" Cooper said angrily. "We need to solve this now."

"We're doing what we can," Annie reminded her. "Besides, now we have Dan helping out a little. Maybe he'll come up with something."

Cooper started to say something, but all of a sudden her mouth was filled with the oily taste she knew so well from her past visions. At the same time, a bright light filled her rearview mirror, as if someone had suddenly turned on a lamp.

"Someone's behind us," Kate said, looking over her shoulder.

The lights shot forward, filling the interior of the Nash with brightness. Cooper was blinded. She tried to see where she was going, but she couldn't.

"They're doing it on purpose!" Annie shouted. "They're trying to run us off the road."

The car behind them was right on their tail, forcing Cooper to go faster and faster on the slick dirt road. Cooper gripped the wheel tightly, trying to will the car to go where she wanted it to. But the other car was forcing her ahead, its headlights confusing her as she tried to see through the driving rain.

All of a sudden a tree loomed out of the darkness in front of them. They were headed right for it, and Cooper knew that if she kept going forward she would smash directly into it.

"Hold on!" she yelled.

Jerking the wheel to the left, she aimed the Nash into the darkness at the side of the road. The car lurched forward, narrowly missing the tree. Cooper heard Annie and Kate scream as they seemed to fall into emptiness. Then the lights behind them went out, and everything went black.

CHAPTER 15

Cooper was sure her parents would kill her. That's why she couldn't tell them about being run off the road. If she told them that, then she would have to tell them about having visited the house by the lake. And if she told them *that*, then she would have to tell them she was still trying to figure out who killed Elizabeth Sanger. So she would have to come up with a different story.

The car had gone down a steep bank and ended up in a field that ran along the side of the road. But it had missed the tree completely. Amazingly, none of them had been seriously hurt. Apart from some bruises from being thrown around a little, they were all fine.

The car was a different story. Although it had started up again on the first try after they'd pushed it out of the grass in the field, there was some noticeable damage. One of the headlights had been smashed, and the paint was scratched in several places. In the dark these things didn't look too bad, but Cooper knew that as soon as her parents saw the car in the daylight they would notice it was no longer in perfect condition. She wasn't sure what she was going to tell them. She had a friend from school who did body work on cars, and she was pretty sure she would be able to fix the Nash, but Cooper would have to wait and see.

In the meantime, they had bigger problems, like figuring out who had tried to run them off the road. What had happened back on the lake road had not been an accident; Cooper knew that. Someone had been waiting for them and had wanted them to crash into that tree. But who? That's the topic they were debating as they drove back to town.

"No one knew we were going there," Annie said. "At least, I didn't tell anyone. Did you guys?"

"Not me," Kate said. "Who would I tell?"

"I sure didn't say anything," Cooper said. "But someone knew."

"Whoever it was must have followed us," said Annie.

"But why wait until we were coming back?" Kate asked. "If somebody wanted us dead, why not just kill us in the house?"

"Maybe he was just trying to scare us?" Annie suggested.

Cooper shook her head. "That was no scare tactic. That car meant business. It tried to push us right into that tree."

"Like I said," Kate commented, "why wait until we were coming back?"

"To make it look like an accident," Cooper said. "If the person driving that car really is connected to Elizabeth's death, then he wouldn't want people to think our deaths were connected to hers. He'd want it to look like a bunch of girls out for a joy ride and going too fast."

"You keep saying 'he,'" said Kate. "It could just as easily have been a woman."

"Like who?" Cooper asked.

"What about Amanda Barclay?" Annie suggested. "She's been on your tail since this whole thing started. What if she has more to do with this than she's letting on?"

"It would certainly explain how she knows all of this insider information," Kate said.

Cooper thought about it for a minute. Was Amanda Barclay capable of murder? She certainly *was* ruthless, and she probably would do just about anything to advance her career. But why would she have killed Elizabeth Sanger?

"I don't think it was her," Cooper said. "But it was definitely someone who thinks we know something we shouldn't."

"Do you think it was the person who killed Elizabeth?" Annie asked quietly.

"Yeah," said Cooper. "I do." She looked over at Annie, and in the harsh light of the street lamps she saw the look of worry on her friend's face.

"You really were hoping it was Barrons, weren't you?" Cooper asked.

"I guess maybe I was," Annie admitted. "It would have made things easier. Now I know that whoever killed Elizabeth really is still out there."

"*Now* do we go to the police?" Kate asked.

There was a long silence as they all thought about what was happening. Finally, Cooper spoke. "I don't think we should," she said. "The only real evidence we have is my visions, and you know how they feel about those."

"But someone tried to kill us!" Kate said.

"But he didn't," Cooper said. "And if we're careful, something like that will never happen again. We just need time. I just need to have one more vision so I can ask Elizabeth who her murderer is. Then we can go to the police. I know I can do it."

She could feel her friends staring at her as she drove.

"Okay," Kate said. "But if anything like this happens again—and I mean *anything*—I'll call Detective Stern myself."

"Deal," Cooper said. "Annie?"

"I don't like it," Annie said. "But I guess you're right. Deal."

"Good," said Cooper. "Now, let's get home."

They drove to Annie's house, where they were supposed to be having a sleepover. After parking the Nash on the street in front of the house, they went inside. Annie's aunt was in the kitchen when they entered.

"What happened to you three?" she asked, noting their wet and dirty clothing. They'd had to push the Nash out of the field and onto another road, and they were wearing the signs of their efforts.

"Oh, we decided to take a little walk," Annie said. "The rain caught us before we could get back to the car."

"A likely story," her aunt replied. "But since the police haven't called and no one is in the hospital, I'm not going to push it. Go get dried off. There's cocoa waiting for you when you're ready."

The girls went up to Annie's attic bedroom and changed into dry things. Back in the kitchen, they poured hot chocolate into mugs and went back upstairs. Cooper settled herself on one of the cushions that sat on Annie's floor, while Annie leaned against the headboard of her big brass bed and Kate flopped at the foot of it.

"Do you think this would have happened if we weren't studying Wicca?" Kate asked suddenly.

Cooper held her mug in her hands, feeling the warmth. "I've been thinking about that," she said.

"And?" asked Annie.

"I don't think it would have," Cooper said. "I mean, I think Elizabeth would have been killed. But I don't think I would have had those visions."

"Do you wish you hadn't?" Annie said.

That question was harder to answer. Did Cooper

wish she'd never seen the things she'd seen? Sometimes. But if she hadn't, then it probably would have been a long time before Elizabeth's body had been found.

"No," Cooper said. "I'm glad it happened. I'm glad I could help a little. Maybe someone else would have had the visions, but maybe not. Maybe I'm the only one who has whatever connection I have with Elizabeth."

"Sometimes I worry that we're opening up a big box that we won't be able to shut again," Kate said carefully. "It seems like as soon as we started playing around with magic, all of these weird things started happening."

"I think we *have* opened something," said Annie. "I think we've opened ourselves to parts of the world—and to parts of ourselves—that we'd kept shut up. Isn't that what witchcraft is all about, opening yourself up to the things around you?"

"I guess," Kate said. "I just wish some of those things weren't so hard."

"Remember the dedication ceremony?" Cooper asked her friends. "They told us that our journeys weren't always going to be easy."

"But they didn't tell us that people would try to kill us," Kate protested.

Cooper ignored Kate. "They also told us that sometimes our paths would cross," she said. "And that sometimes we would travel together and sometimes we would travel on our own. I think this is what they meant."

"What do you mean?" Annie asked.

"I think my path and Elizabeth's path crossed for some reason," Cooper explained. "I don't know why she died. But for some reason, I've been brought into her journey and she's been brought into mine, if that makes any sense."

"And you dragged us along with you," Kate added. "Thanks a lot."

"That's part of it too," Cooper said, trying to explain what she was thinking—and afraid she wasn't doing a very good job of it. "Maybe my path is to learn to use these visions. Elizabeth's death provided an opportunity for that. I don't mean that she died so that I could learn some kind of lesson or anything. It just worked out that way. And maybe my payment, or whatever you want to call it, for learning the lesson is to help her."

"And how exactly do Annie and I fit into it again?" Kate said.

"Sorry," Cooper answered. "You'll have to figure that out for yourselves. But I do think all of this stuff is happening to show me something. To show *us* something."

"I guess I always just thought about magic in terms of good things," Kate said. "Like getting three wishes and changing toads into princes. That kind of thing."

"That's what got you into trouble in the first

place, remember?" Annie said. "You know magic isn't like that. It's like Sophia says, you can't have dark without light, or night without day."

"I know," Kate said, sighing. "But I wish we'd get more enchanted toads and fewer maniac drivers."

"You've got your toad," Cooper teased. "Why do you need another one?"

"Where is Tyler tonight anyway?" Annie asked Kate.

"Doing some coven thing," Kate answered. "You know, one of those hush-hush, secret things none of us baby witches-in-training are allowed to know about yet."

"Whatever they're doing, I doubt it's half as interesting as our evening," Annie said. "I'm beat."

They were all exhausted, so they went to bed. There were still many unanswered questions floating around in Cooper's head, but she fell asleep quickly. The next thing she knew, Annie's aunt was knocking on the door and telling them it was time for breakfast.

Ten minutes later Cooper was in the kitchen. As she sat down, she noticed the headline on the Sunday paper Annie's aunt had placed on the table: PROSECUTORS DECIDE TO ASK FOR DEATH. Below it was a picture of Christopher Barrons. Cooper picked up the paper and quickly read the article.

Prosecutors in the murder case against Christopher Barrons have decided to ask for the death penalty. "We feel we have enough

evidence to prove that Christopher Barrons did, in fact, murder Elizabeth Sanger," said District Attorney Jerry Muller. "Given the nature of the murder, we also feel that it warrants the death penalty," Muller said, referring to the fact that Sanger, 15, was strangled.

Cooper didn't bother to read the rest of the article. She hadn't known how Elizabeth died. Someone had strangled her. Cooper couldn't even imagine how horrible that must have been. And she knew a lot of other people would be thinking the same thing. All she could think about was that unless something was done, and quickly, Christopher Barrons would probably be tried, convicted, and sentenced to death.

"What's wrong?" Annie asked, noticing the strange look on Cooper's face.

Cooper showed her and Kate the newspaper. They read the article.

"We have to do something," Cooper said. "Someone has got to know *something*." She thought hard, going over everything she knew about Elizabeth's murder.

Kate was reading the article a second time. "Poor Arthur Perch," she said. "First his wife, and now this. He'll never go back to that house now."

"What did you say?" Cooper asked.

"Arthur Perch," Kate repeated. "It's his house where all these things happened, remember?"

"Annie, do you have a phone book?" Cooper asked.

"Sure," Annie replied. "Why?"

"Just get it," Cooper said. "Please."

Annie brought her the phone book. Cooper flopped it open and wordlessly began turning pages. When she found the page she was looking for she ran her finger down the column, stopped, then grabbed the phone and dialed.

"Who are you calling?" Kate asked, but Cooper shushed her.

"Hello?" a voice on the other end said.

"Mr. Perch?" Cooper asked. "This is Cooper Rivers."

"Cooper who?" the man said.

"Rivers," Cooper said. "I'm the one who led police to your house, where Elizabeth Sanger was murdered."

"Oh, yes," Mr. Perch replied. "I read about you in the papers. That's a strange story. But what can I do for you?"

"Mr. Perch, I know this will sound weird, but can I ask you a question?"

"I suppose so," he said.

"Does anyone else have a key to the house?" Cooper asked. "Besides yourself, I mean."

Mr. Perch sighed. "That house has been locked up since the day of Martha's funeral," he said sadly. "Locked it myself. And I've never been back."

"You locked it when you left?" Cooper repeated.

"Yes," he replied.

"Does anyone else have a key?" asked Cooper. "I know it's a strange question, but it's important. I'll explain in a minute."

"That was a long time ago," Mr. Perch said. "I haven't thought about that summer in quite some time. But as I recall, the only people at the house that summer were me and Martha. Our children were all away."

"So it was just the two of you?" Cooper said, her hopes fading.

"Oh, and the boy," Mr. Perch said. "He was there."

"The boy?" Cooper said.

"Yes," said Mr. Perch. "Martha hired a young man to do odd jobs around the place that summer. Fix windows. Replace some rotted boards on the porch. That kind of thing."

"And did he have a key?" Cooper pressed.

"A key?" Mr. Perch said, sounding confused. "Well, yes, I guess he would have had a key. He would have needed to go in and out from time to time."

"And did you get it back when you left?" asked Cooper.

"I'm not sure that I did," the man answered. "There was a lot going on then, you see. I don't think getting the key back from Dan was really one of the things on my mind."

"Dan?" said Cooper.

"Funny that I remember his name," Mr. Perch said. "Just came to me right then. But Dan it was. Local boy. Our son knew him from school or some such thing. Dan Hutchins, was it? Something like that."

"Was it Huctwith?" Cooper asked, her heart starting to beat quickly in her chest.

"Huctwith," Mr. Perch said. "Yes, that was it. Dan Huctwith. How did you know that?"

"I know his sister," Cooper answered. "Mr. Perch, thank you for talking to me. I really appreciate it."

"The pleasure's mine," the man replied. "But you still haven't told me what made you call me."

"Just a hunch," Cooper answered.

"Well, I hope I was helpful."

"You were more helpful than I ever could have hoped," Cooper answered. "Thank you. Thank you very much."

She hung up the phone.

"Well?" Annie asked.

Cooper looked at her friends. "I think I know who killed Elizabeth," she said.

CHAPTER 16

"Where is she?" Cooper said for the third time. "We told her five o'clock."

"Maybe she had to do something for her aunt after school," Kate replied. "It's only five-thirty now anyway."

"It's not like Annie to be late," said Cooper. "If anything, she's always early."

They were sitting in Cooper's bedroom on Monday afternoon, waiting for Annie to arrive so they could decide what to do next. Ever since talking to Arthur Perch the day before, Cooper had been trying to put all of the pieces of the puzzle together. She'd gone over and over everything a thousand times, and still it didn't make sense.

"I just don't understand why Dan would kill Elizabeth," Kate said, voicing the one question that had been troubling all of them the most.

"I don't know why," Cooper responded. "I'm just sure that he did." It's what she'd been telling her friends ever since she'd first told them of her suspicions.

"Run down this theory for me one more time," Kate said.

Cooper sighed. They'd already gone over this numerous times. "I thought we were waiting for Annie," she said.

"Please," said Kate. "She's probably made flow-charts for us to look at. I, on the other hand, am still confused. So humor me."

Cooper rearranged herself on the bed. "Okay," she said. "Dan worked for the Perches the summer Mrs. Perch died, right?"

Kate nodded.

"So he had a key to the house," Cooper explained. "That would explain why the house wasn't broken into when Elizabeth was taken there. The murderer used a key. Dan's key."

"But he worked there a long time ago," Kate said. "He could have lost that key or given it to someone. Christopher Barrons might even have stolen it, for all we know."

"True," said Cooper. "But the key isn't the only thing. Remember the footprints in the dust?"

"Sure," Kate answered. "You only made us look at them for about an hour. Why?"

"Well, remember that I said something about the pattern being familiar?"

Again Kate nodded. "But you didn't know why," she said.

"I do now," replied Cooper. "Look."

She held up one of her feet.

"*You* made those prints?" Kate asked, confused.

"No," said Cooper, wiggling one of her feet. "But these did."

Kate looked at Cooper's foot. She was wearing her favorite pair of old Doc Martens.

"Check out the tread on these," Cooper told her friend. "See the parallel lines? That's almost the same pattern that the killer's footprints have."

"Again, so what?" Kate said. "A lot of people wear Doc Martens."

"Not like those," Cooper said, shaking her head. "See how the tread on my boots is worn down? The patterns in the footprints came from a new pair of boots. And not just any boots—the newest design. The only place I've seen those boots for sale is Alice's Attic. And the only person I've seen wearing a pair is Dan Huctwith. I noticed them the first time we met him, because I thought they were really cool."

Kate groaned. "But you can't prove that he's the only person in Beecher Falls with those boots," she said. "I know this all *looks* bad, but you have to admit that it doesn't *prove* anything."

"It's not just the key and the boots," Cooper said. "Dan knew Elizabeth. He had a lot of opportunities to be around her."

Kate gave her a look. "So did a lot of other people."

Cooper was becoming more and more frustrated. "Do you *want* Christopher Barrons to die?" she asked angrily.

"No," said Kate. "No more than you do. But the police already think you're a little off the deep end. If you go in there telling them that you know Dan Huctwith killed Elizabeth but you can't really prove it, they're going to laugh you out of the station. They just want this case over with. If you're going to convince them that they have the wrong guy, you need to give them something more than just a few suspicions."

Cooper wanted to say something in her defense, but she knew that Kate was right. People did think she was weird. Detective Stern had been thankful for her help in finding Elizabeth's body, but that was because she'd led him to something he could see. When it came to suspecting Dan Huctwith of Elizabeth's murder, all she had to give the police were some iffy clues. She needed that one final piece of evidence that would convince them that she was right.

The phone rang, and Cooper got up. "Maybe it's Annie calling to tell us she's on her way," she said as she picked it up. "Hello?"

"Hello, Cooper," said a man's voice.

"Who is this?" Cooper asked, ready to hang up in case it was another one of the prank calls she'd been getting off and on since the story naming her ran in the paper.

"It's Dan," the man said. "You remember me from Alice's Attic, don't you?"

Cooper felt her throat tighten. Why was Dan calling her? She didn't know what to say. She didn't want him to think that she was suspicious of him, so she tried to calm herself so she'd sound normal when she finally spoke.

"Oh, hi," she said, hoping she sounded casual. "What's up?"

"I told you I'd call if I found out anything," Dan said.

"Right," Cooper said. "So, did you find something?"

Dan laughed. "You might say that," he said.

"Great," Cooper replied. "What is it?"

"Here," Dan said. "I'll let you hear for yourself."

Cooper heard him moving the phone around. There was some rustling, and then another voice came on the line. "Cooper?"

"Annie?" Cooper said, recognizing her friend's voice. "Where are you?" A coldness had suddenly washed over her.

There was more rustling, and then Dan came back on. "Annie's fine," he said calmly. "She and I are having a little chat."

"What are you doing with her?" Cooper demanded furiously.

"Now, calm down," Dan said. "There's no need to get unpleasant."

"You killed Elizabeth, didn't you?" Cooper said.

She looked over at Kate, who was beginning to understand what was happening from listening to Cooper's end of the conversation. There was a look of horror on Kate's face.

Dan paused. "Well, you certainly do get right to the point," he said, sounding irritated.

"Well, did you?" Cooper asked again.

"Maybe I did," Dan responded. "And maybe I didn't. That's not what I called to chat about."

"Then, what do you want?"

Dan gave a long sigh. "It seems that despite all the evidence to the contrary, you *do* think that I killed Elizabeth. Isn't that right?"

"Yes," said Cooper simply. "I do."

"But the police don't," Dan said. "The public doesn't. And Amanda Barclay doesn't."

"Maybe because you've been feeding her false information," Cooper said, laying out one of her cards. She wasn't sure it was Dan who had been calling Amanda from the pay phone, but she suspected as much.

"From what I understand, all of that information came from an anonymous source," Dan answered coolly.

Cooper had no answer for him, so she kept quiet. A moment later, Dan continued.

"It seems the only people who think I had anything to do with Elizabeth's death are three teenage girls, one of whom is just a little bit nuts and says she talks to ghosts."

Cooper felt her anger rising. Dan was playing with her, trying to make her say or do something stupid. "That ghost showed me where you left her body," she said evenly.

"Lucky guess," said Dan. "But you're missing the point."

"Which is?" asked Cooper.

"You're the one putting doubts into people's minds," Dan said. "You can just as easily make them think that what they believe is true."

"You mean that Christopher Barrons really did kill Elizabeth?" said Cooper.

"Very good," Dan replied. "That's exactly what I mean."

"And how do I do that?" asked Cooper.

"Do another interview with Amanda Barclay," Dan said. "Tell her that you've had another vision or whatever it is you have. Tell her that Elizabeth's ghost told you that Barrons really did kill her."

"But he didn't," said Cooper stubbornly.

"People think he did," Dan responded. "Let them keep thinking that. What difference does it make if one homeless bum disappears?"

"But you killed Elizabeth," Cooper said. "Not Barrons."

"No one is going to believe I did it," Dan said. "After all, what motive would I have?"

He had Cooper there. It was the one thing she couldn't figure out at all. Dan really didn't seem to have any motive whatsoever for killing Elizabeth.

"See," said Dan smugly. "Even you know I'm innocent."

"What are you doing with Annie if you're so innocent?" Cooper shot back. "Why did you kidnap her?"

Dan laughed again. "I didn't kidnap her," he said. "I just borrowed her for a little while. She's my insurance. I'm going to keep her here with me until I'm sure you've given Amanda Barclay your final interview. Once it runs, I'll let her go."

"And what's to stop me from telling the police everything once she's free?" asked Cooper. "This doesn't sound like a very good plan to me."

"Oh, but it is," Dan answered. "Did you really think I wouldn't expect you to do that? I don't care if you go to the police. Tell them anything you want to. By that point I'll be long gone. They might look around a little bit, but everyone will still think that Barrons did it. They'll need someone to blame this on, because people will want to believe everything has been tied up nice and neat. And like I said, who cares if some old drunk goes to the gas chamber? A lot of people think he should have gone there already for killing that first girl."

"That was an accident," Cooper said. "He didn't kill her deliberately."

"People don't care about that," Dan said. "They just need a scapegoat. And trust me, Barrons makes a very good one. Why do you think I picked him?"

"What are you talking about?" asked Cooper.

"You don't think Barrons ended up with all of Elizabeth's stuff by accident, do you?" Dan replied.

"You gave it to him," Cooper said, suddenly understanding. "You gave it to him knowing he would try to sell her jewelry. Then you called Amanda Barclay and told her he'd done it."

"I didn't give it to him," said Dan. "Elizabeth did. She left it with a little note saying she wanted to help him out and suggesting he could pawn the stuff for some money. After all, they were friends, right? At least that's what he told the police. Too bad they didn't believe him."

Cooper couldn't believe what she was hearing. Dan had planned everything down to the last detail. Barrons thought that Elizabeth had given him the necklace as a gift. He didn't know anything about Dan, so he couldn't tell the police about him. No wonder they weren't looking for another suspect. They didn't believe Barrons any more than they would believe Cooper, because he didn't have any proof to back up his story. And Dan had called Amanda Barclay and given her all kinds of information that made Barrons look guilty. Everything Dan did took people another step away from him and closer to Barrons.

"You can tell anyone you want this story," Dan continued. "But I don't think you will."

"And why not?" Cooper asked.

"Because I'll still be out there somewhere," Dan answered. "And as you found out the other night, it's so easy for accidents to happen."

"So you did follow us out to the house," Cooper said. "Nice try. But it didn't work, did it?"

"Next time it might," Dan said. "And I promise you that if you go talking about this, there will be a next time. Three next times, if you understand what I'm saying. But as long as we keep this our little secret, I'll stay out of your way. The Perch woman should have remembered that."

"Martha Perch?" Cooper said. "You killed her?"

"She fell down the stairs," said Dan with fake sincerity. "Slipped and went right down them. I tried calling 911, but it was too late, I'm afraid. She was dead when they got there."

"But why?" Cooper said. It hadn't occurred to her that Dan might have had anything to do with Mrs. Perch's death, but now it made sense.

"She talked too much," he said. "Accused me of stealing money from the house, said she was going to tell her husband. I told her it was better to just forget about everything, that she must be mistaken, but she insisted."

"So you pushed her down the stairs," Cooper said, finishing the story.

"A terrible accident," Dan said. "Poor Arthur was so distraught he never set foot in the house again."

"And Elizabeth?" Cooper asked. "Did she threaten to tell someone something too?"

"Let's just say she knew a little too much," Dan answered. "Talked to some of the wrong people."

"How do I know you won't hurt Annie?" Cooper asked.

"I told you I wouldn't," Dan said. "And I always keep my promises. Besides, I'm a nice guy. You know that."

"Yeah," said Cooper. "Real nice."

Dan laughed. "You can't always trust first impressions," he said. "So, do we have a deal? You'll go talk to Barclay and get an article in the paper. As soon as it appears, I'll let your friend go and be on my way."

Cooper thought hard. She had no idea what to do. Dan had killed Mrs. Perch because she threatened to expose his stealing. He had killed Elizabeth for something similar. She knew he would have no qualms about killing Annie if she didn't do what he was asking her to do.

"Okay," Cooper said. "I'll do it. I'll call Amanda Barclay right now."

"Good girl," Dan said. "As soon as I see the article, I'll let your friend go."

"You'd better not hurt her," Cooper told him. "If you do, I'll hunt you down myself."

"It's almost worth doing just to have you come after me," Dan teased. "Don't tempt me."

He hung up and the line went dead. Cooper stared at the phone for a minute and then put it back.

"What did he say?" Kate asked anxiously. "Is Annie okay?"

"She will be," Cooper said. "She will be."

CHAPTER 17

Cooper sat on the big purple velvet sofa in the back room of Crones' Circle, and Kate sat to her right. Sophia, Robin, and some members of other covens stood and sat around the room.

"He must have gotten her while she was walking to your house," Robin said to Cooper.

After the conversation with Dan Huctwith, Cooper and Kate had run to Crones' Circle, not daring to go to the police and not knowning what else to do.

"So," said Kate after Cooper was done telling everyone what had happened, "what do we do? We have to get Annie away from him, but we can't let him get away with this. Can you help us?"

"We might be able to help," Sophia said. "It all depends on Cooper."

"Me?" said Cooper, surprised to hear Sophia say such a thing. "Why me?"

"Elizabeth came to you when she needed help," Sophia explained. "You're the only one who has been able to communicate with her. If you can reach her again, she might be able to give us information that will help us locate Annie."

"But I haven't been able to do that!" Cooper said, frustrated. "Remember? I fainted the last time she came through. And the last time I tried to contact her, nothing happened."

"Yes," said Sophia. "I know you're a little burned out. But I think that if we all work together to create a circle of protection, you might be able to do it."

"You mean all of you would help me?" Cooper said.

Sophia nodded. "We have a lot of strong witches here," she said. "If we all put our energy into a circle, we might be able to give you the strength and the protection you need to contact Elizabeth again."

"But it's not guaranteed?" Cooper asked.

"No," answered Sophia. "I can't promise that it will work. Magic isn't foolproof."

"Could Cooper be hurt?" said Kate.

"Yes," said Sophia. "There is some risk involved. Cooper has already had some very strong psychic experiences. She's tired. That's why she's been unable to contact Elizabeth again. It's possible that trying this time will cause some pain. She might even destroy completely whatever abilities she has for communicating with the dead."

"You mean I might never be able to do it again?" Cooper asked.

"It could happen," Sophia said. "If the experience is too strong, your mind could shut down that part of itself it uses for such things. If we're going to attempt this, you should understand that."

Kate looked at Cooper. "Do you want to risk that?" she asked.

Cooper smiled. "I didn't ask for any of this in the first place," she said. "Elizabeth came to me and asked me to help her. I don't know why, but I know it's part of what I'm supposed to learn. If it means not ever being able to do it again, then that's okay with me. Besides, Annie is my friend. I'd do anything for her."

Kate took Cooper's hand and held it tightly, not saying anything. She hoped that she would be able to help. But she was nervous. What if whatever Sophia had in mind didn't work? What if Cooper couldn't contact Elizabeth? She hadn't called Amanda Barclay like she'd told Dan she would. There would be no article in the paper the next day. What would Dan do then? She tried not to think about it.

"Let's begin, then," Sophia said. "We need to clear everything out so that we can make a big circle."

Everyone helped move the furniture to the sides of the room. Sophia took several cushions and laid them in the center of the floor.

"Cooper, you will be here," she said. "The rest of us will form a circle around you."

Cooper lay down on the cushions. The others formed a circle, sitting on the floor. She looked around at the women and men gathered in the room. They were all her friends, even the people whose names she didn't know but whose faces she recognized from seeing them at rituals. She trusted them.

Sophia was sitting opposite Cooper's head, with Thatcher on one side and Rowan, Tyler's mother, on the other. She was holding an unlit white candle in her hands. "Please turn off the lights," she said.

Someone switched off the lights, and the room was plunged into darkness. Cooper could feel the people around her, circling her protectively, and she felt safe. But she was still frightened. What if nothing happened? She didn't want to disappoint everyone. Especially Annie.

"Try not to think about anything worrisome," Sophia said gently through the darkness. "I know that's hard, but you need to be as relaxed as possible. Feel the cushions beneath you, supporting you. Let your body sink into them."

Cooper did as Sophia instructed. She felt herself resting on the cushions, and she tried to let the tension flow out of her.

"The rest of you are going to picture yourselves

drawing light up from the earth," Sophia said. "Imagine it flowing up into your body, filling you completely. Feel it flowing through your veins. When you feel ready, let the light pass through your fingers and spread out, connecting with the light of those around you and forming a circle around Cooper."

There was silence as everyone focused their thoughts. Cooper imagined them all filled with light, creating a circle of whiteness around her in the dark room. She imagined the light pulsing with energy and power, keeping out anything that might try to harm her or break her concentration.

"Our circle is cast," Sophia said after a few minutes. "Cooper, you are between the worlds, in a safe place. We will hold the circle strong while you go in search of Elizabeth. I'm going to light the candle now. Focus your thoughts on the flame. Call to Elizabeth."

Cooper saw fire spark up and die down as Sophia held a match to the candle. The flame danced brightly, flickering across the circle. Cooper took a deep breath and focused on the center of the fire, where the orange and yellow blurred into a tiny, bright eye.

Here goes nothing, she thought to herself.

"See the flame as a doorway," Sophia said.

Cooper gazed at the fire, letting all her other thoughts fall away. It was hard. She kept having random thoughts. Where was Annie? Was she okay? Why had Dan killed Elizabeth? Maybe they should have gone to the police. All of these things flashed through her mind.

She tried to block out everything except the fire. She let it fill her vision, imagined it leaping up and becoming as tall as she was. She imagined standing in front of it the way she had stood in front of the door in the lake house.

"Elizabeth," she called out in her mind. "Elizabeth. Can you hear me? I need your help. Please. Annie is in trouble."

She waited, but nothing seemed to be happening. Some part of her was still holding back, afraid that if she let go completely she would find herself fainting again, or worse.

"Let go." Sophia's voice floated through her thoughts. "Let us hold you. Remember the connections."

The connections. Cooper thought about the word she had chosen during her dedication ritual. She thought about her connections to the people in the room, to Annie, and to Elizabeth. She imagined herself connected to them by a network of golden light, a network that both tied her to them and also created a safety net in case she should fall.

You have to let go, she told herself. *You have to risk falling again.*

She was afraid. But she knew she had to do it. She had to believe that the people around her wouldn't let her fall. She took another deep breath and let go. She let herself sink into the fire in Sophia's hands. She let it slip around her, consuming her.

"I'm here." Elizabeth's voice was loud and clear.

Cooper looked up. Standing in the circle with her was Elizabeth, looking just as she had looked all the other times. Seeing her, Cooper wanted to cry out in happiness. She'd come through.

"I've been trying to talk to you," she said to Elizabeth.

"I know," the girl replied. "I've tried to get through too, but something was blocking me, keeping me out."

"That was me," Cooper said, ashamed. "I was afraid."

Elizabeth smiled a small, sad smile. "I know what that's like," she said.

"Dan Huctwith killed you, didn't he?" Cooper asked.

Elizabeth nodded. "Yes," she said. "When I saw him at the service, I felt the anger and the fear rising off him, and I knew."

"Do you remember anything more?" Cooper asked.

"A little," Elizabeth said. "I remember going to the store. I remember starting to leave. Then it all goes black until the house."

"He must have knocked you out somehow,"

Cooper said, remembering the strange taste in her mouth. "Do you remember him—" She couldn't finish the sentence.

"Killing me?" Elizabeth said. "Yes, I remember that. I remember trying to scream, and him putting his hands on my throat. Then everything went black again. When I woke up again I was in the dark place, wandering around. I called and called for help, but no one came. I thought I was in the house again. Then I called again, and suddenly I saw you sleeping. I tried to wake you up."

"That's when my dreams began," Cooper said.

"I kept trying to wake you," Elizabeth continued. "But every time you woke up, I found myself back in the dark place again. Until that night in the fire."

"Dan said he killed you because you knew too much," Cooper said. "What was he talking about?"

Elizabeth looked confused. "I thought he was joking," she said.

"Who was joking?" Cooper asked. "Dan?"

Elizabeth shook her head. "Johnny. One of the kids on the street. He and I used to talk a lot. He was really sweet. His parents kicked him out of the house for some reason. I forget why. I used to give him lunch sometimes. Dan used to hang out with him too. One day we were talking and Johnny told me that one night when he and Dan had gone out drinking together Dan had gotten drunk and confessed that he'd killed an old woman. I thought Johnny was just making up the story to mess with me. He liked to do that—make up stories. Anyway, when I went back to work I told Dan what Johnny had said. I thought he would think it was funny. He laughed about it and said he'd told Johnny the story to see if he would believe it. I thought that was the end of it."

"But he really had killed an old woman," Cooper said. "Mrs. Perch, the wife of the man who owns the house where you were murdered. He must have been so drunk he didn't remember telling Johnny about it."

Elizabeth shook her head. "Then he probably killed Johnny too," she said. "A few days before Dan killed me, Johnny disappeared. No one knew where he was. Dan told me that Johnny had come by the store and said he was leaving town for a while. I bet Dan killed him so he wouldn't talk."

"And then he killed you to make sure no one was left who knew that he had killed Martha Perch," Cooper said.

"Now it makes sense," Elizabeth said. "He was afraid that I really did know about it. I didn't know what I'd done to make him kill me."

"You didn't do anything," Cooper said. "And we're going to make sure Dan gets caught. But first we have to find him and Annie. Do you have any idea where they are?"

"I can try," Elizabeth said. "Sometimes when I

concentrate I can feel his rage. It burns me like fire, so I don't do it very often. It's the same with you. I was able to find you because I could sense your anger."

"Do I burn you too?" Cooper asked, afraid that she was causing Elizabeth pain.

"No," the other girl said. "Your anger is healing. It's good anger, the kind that comes from wanting to help people. That's what attracted me to you in the first place."

Hearing Elizabeth say that made Cooper feel good about herself. She'd never really thought about her anger as a strength before. It had always seemed like a weakness to her, something that prevented her from getting to know people. But maybe she just had to learn when to use her anger in a positive way. And now was a good time to start.

"Can you help me find where Dan is keeping Annie, then?" she asked Elizabeth.

Elizabeth closed her eyes. As Cooper watched, the other girl suddenly doubled over in pain, her hands holding her head. Cooper stepped forward and grabbed her, once again feeling how cold she was to touch. But she held on as Elizabeth twitched with pain and her breath came in ragged gasps.

"A warehouse," Elizabeth said. "Near the store. No one uses it. He has her in a back room. She's afraid."

"Can you tell me exactly where it is?" Cooper said.

Elizabeth groaned again as another wave of pain overtook her. "There's a sign out front," she said faintly. "Gleason's Plumbing. It's very faded, but you'll be able to see it."

Elizabeth stiffened and fell limp in Cooper's arms. She was breathing, but irregularly, and her eyes were closed. Cooper held her, feeling the coldness of her skin and wondering what she must be feeling inside. Was it the same way Cooper had felt when she sensed Elizabeth's fear and rage in the synagogue?

"Go," Elizabeth said weakly. "Go find Annie. Stop Dan from hurting anyone else."

"What about you?" Cooper asked. "What will happen to you?"

"I don't know," said Elizabeth. "But I know this is what you're supposed to do."

As Cooper watched, Elizabeth faded out. She seemed to dissolve into the air like mist, leaving Cooper alone. "Elizabeth!" she called out, trying to get her to return. "Elizabeth!"

She felt someone touching her. "Elizabeth?" she said.

"No," said a woman's voice. "It's Sophia."

Cooper looked around. She was still lying on the cushions. Sophia was kneeling next to her, holding her hand.

"You found her, didn't you?" she asked Cooper.

Cooper nodded. "She told me where Annie is," she said.

Sophia smiled. "I knew you could do it," she said.

Cooper sighed. "I'm glad one of us did."

CHAPTER 18

"You're sure this is the place?"

Detective Stern stood in front of the old warehouse, looking up at the faded sign for Gleason's Plumbing. The lights around the sign had been smashed long before, but the lettering was still readable in the glare of the street lamps.

"That's it," Cooper told him.

"And tell me again how you know this guy has your friend in there?" the detective asked.

"The same way I knew Elizabeth's body was in the house by the lake," Cooper answered.

"More ghosts," the detective muttered.

"Just one," Cooper replied, watching him frown.

They had called the detective as soon as Cooper had come out of her trance. Cooper hadn't told him the whole story, just that Dan Huctwith was holding Annie hostage in a warehouse. The detective had been furious at her for not calling him sooner, and he had ordered everyone except Cooper to stay at Crones' Circle, then he sent an officer to Annie's house to tell her Aunt Sarah what was going on. He needed Cooper's help to find the warehouse.

"Why can't anything about this case be normal?" the detective said.

An unmarked car with three other officers in it was parked down the street. They hadn't wanted to give Dan Huctwith any warning that they were on to him. As far as Dan knew, Cooper was sitting somewhere with Amanda Barclay, spilling her guts about how she'd made a mistake when she'd insisted that Christopher Barrons wasn't the murderer.

Detective Stern motioned toward the car, and the officers got out. Keeping to the shadows, they walked along the street to where Cooper and the detective stood.

"The front door is locked," Stern pointed out. "We're going to have to go in the back way. And we're going to have to try not to make any noise. If he hears us, he might do anything."

The officers began to creep around the side of the building, their guns drawn. Detective Stern turned to Cooper. "You go sit in the car," he said. "Lock the doors. If Huctwith comes out, you duck down and stay there. Got it?"

Cooper nodded. She started walking toward the car. Stern watched until he was sure she was getting in, then he followed the officers into the alley that ran alongside the warehouse. As soon as he was out of sight, Cooper reversed directions.

She knew following the officers was stupid, but it was her friend in there. She wasn't going to just sit in the car and wait.

She couldn't see the policemen anywhere in the dark alley, and figured that they must be at the rear of the warehouse, looking for a way in. She continued to walk down the alley, ignoring the smell and the rats that darted in and out of the shadows as she passed by. She hoped Annie was okay.

When she was almost at the end of the alley, she passed another door. It was open a crack, as if the officers had already tried it. Cooper pulled on the handle, but something was blocking the door, and it wouldn't open any wider. There wasn't enough room for a man to get through. *But I bet I could get in there,* Cooper thought.

She put one foot into the crack and followed it with one shoulder. It was a tight squeeze. She felt the rusty metal scraping her skin as she pushed her way inside the warehouse, trying to not make any noise. When half of her body was through, she got stuck, and for a moment she couldn't move in either direction. But then she held her breath, gave one last push, and found herself on the inside.

The room she was in was filled with boxes. Old pipes and fittings were scattered all over the floor, and everything was covered with dust and cobwebs. There was only one small window set high in the wall, but it let in just enough light from a nearby street lamp for Cooper to make her way through the trash to the doorway on the other side of the room.

She looked out and saw the large main floor of the warehouse. It too was filled with lots of boxes and old plumbing supplies. More light from the street lamps came in through the cracked and filthy windows, but the space was still murky. It was also eerily silent, and Cooper wondered if Elizabeth had been mistaken. There didn't seem to be anyone in the place at all.

Then she heard a sound. At the rear of the warehouse, a set of stairs went up to a platform. There was a door there, and Cooper guessed that there was some kind of office behind it. The door was opening, and a moment later she saw a dark figure come out and stand on the platform, looking out into the cavernous warehouse. It was Dan. Cooper ducked behind a pile of boxes so that he couldn't possibly see her in the dim light of the street lamps.

Where are the cops? she wondered. *Why aren't they in here yet?* She listened for any sign that they had found a way into the warehouse, hoping they would burst out of the shadows and capture Dan. But nothing happened.

She looked out from behind the pile of boxes. Dan had shut the office door and was walking down the stairs. He disappeared into the shadows. Cooper wondered where he was going. Was he leaving the warehouse? If so, was Annie in the room he'd just left?

Cooper's heart raced as she tried to decide what to do. The rational part of her told her to just wait right there and let the police handle everything. But another part of her told her to go see if her friend really was in the room. But what if she was? How would Cooper get her out? What if Dan came back and caught them? Cooper had no idea where he was going or how long he might be gone. For all she knew, he was still there, sitting in the shadows and waiting for someone to do something stupid like try to rescue Annie.

Please hurry up, she thought, trying to will the police to appear. But they didn't. And every second she waited was another second lost. Dan could come back at any moment. This was her only chance.

She crept toward the office, trying to stay hidden behind the boxes. A moment later she was standing across from the stairs. There was about twenty feet of wide-open space between her hiding place and the steps, and she would have to make a run for it.

She ran, waiting for Dan to leap out and stop her. But he didn't, and a few seconds later she was standing in front of the office door. She tried the knob, and it turned. Her heart beating wildly, she opened the door.

Annie was inside, sitting in a chair opposite a dusty desk scattered with empty styrofoam coffee cups and pieces of paper. Her hands were tied behind her, and there was tape over her mouth. When she saw Cooper standing in the doorway, her eyes went wide. Cooper ran over and pulled the tape from her friend's mouth.

"How did you find me?" Annie asked.

"Quiet," Cooper whispered. "I don't know when Dan will be back."

She went behind the chair and worked at the knots in the rope that bound Annie's hands. In the dim light, she saw that her friend's feet were similarly tied. The knots were tight, and Cooper was having a hard time working them free.

"He told me he was going to let me go if you did what he told you to," Annie said.

"Yeah," said Cooper. "I know. But there was a change of plans."

"Really?" said a voice. Dan's voice.

Cooper looked up. Dan was standing in the doorway of the office, smirking at them.

"So, you decided to play superhero," he said. "That's too bad. Didn't I tell you what would happen if you didn't stick with the original plan?"

Cooper put her hands on Annie's shoulders. "I didn't tell anyone," she said.

Dan laughed. "I guess not," he said. "Otherwise you wouldn't be standing there by yourself."

Where's Stern? Cooper thought. She wasn't about to tell Dan that there were police coming. If he knew that, he might do something drastic. She had to play the game out until the cops could get into the warehouse. Why hadn't she listened to Stern and just stayed in the car?

"There is something I'm curious about, though," Dan said. "How did you know I was here?"

"Elizabeth told me," Cooper answered, figuring there was no point in trying to lie. "She also told me that you killed Johnny."

Dan's smile faded. He took a step toward the girls. "Elizabeth doesn't know anything about that," he said.

"Yes, she does," Cooper said, trying to sound confident. "And now I know it. You killed her because you thought she knew about Martha Perch. But she didn't. She thought you and Johnny were playing a joke on her."

"She was going to tell someone," Dan snarled. "I had to make sure she didn't. And now I have to make sure the two of you don't tell anyone, either."

He pulled a gun from his waistband and pointed it at Cooper and Annie. Cooper felt Annie stiffen in fear. She herself felt as if she might collapse. She'd never seen a real gun before, and definitely not one that was being pointed straight at her by a person who wanted her dead more than he wanted anything else in the world.

"You should have kept quiet," Dan said, stepping closer. "You should have kept your stupid visions to yourself."

"Elizabeth needed my help," Cooper said. "She

also knew Barrons didn't kill her."

"But no one else will ever know that," Dan said. "At least, not after I'm done with the two of you. Now, who goes first? I don't suppose it really matters, since you'll be able to talk to each other when you're ghosts anyway."

He laughed. Cooper wanted to kill him. She wished she could somehow hurt Dan the way he had hurt other people. It wasn't fair. Martha Perch hadn't done anything. Neither had Johnny or Elizabeth. They'd just known things Dan wanted to keep secret, and he had killed them for it. Cooper felt powerless, standing there with the gun aimed at her and Annie, and that made her angrier than she'd ever been. She felt the fire of her rage burning inside her, filling her mind.

The air between Cooper and Dan shimmered as if an invisible flame were burning there. Cooper stared at it, watching Dan's face contort behind the rippling waves of energy. She could see an expression of confusion on his face.

"What the hell are you doing?" he demanded.

But Cooper wasn't doing anything. She watched, wondering, as the air thickened and a shape took form. A moment later Elizabeth was standing there, facing Dan, her back to Cooper and Annie.

"Why, Dan?" she said. "Why did you kill me?"

Dan backed away, the gun in his hand moving from side to side. Cooper prayed that he wouldn't fire it.

"Get away from me!" he yelled. "Get away. You're not real."

"I'm real," Elizabeth said. "As real as the night you strangled me in that house while I begged you to stop."

She stepped forward, sending Dan scrambling backward another step. Elizabeth kept going. Dan turned and dashed for the door. Elizabeth seemed to run after him then, and she reached out, her pale arms going around his body. Cooper heard Dan scream, and then there was a dull sound, like something had hit the warehouse floor. Cooper ran to the door. Elizabeth was standing on the platform, looking down. Cooper saw Dan's body lying at the foot of the stairs, one of his legs bent at an odd angle. He was moaning.

A moment later, Cooper heard a crash and the sound of footsteps. Detective Stern and the other officers rushed into the warehouse, waving flashlights and guns. When they saw Dan lying on the floor, two of them ran over and handcuffed him while the third snatched the gun, which he'd dropped during his fall.

Detective Stern ran up the steps and stopped in front of Cooper. "I thought I told you to stay in the car," he said angrily.

"I know. I know," Cooper said. "But I didn't see you guys exactly storming the place."

"The doors were all locked and barricaded," Stern said.

"Not the one in the alley," Cooper said.

"We couldn't fit through it," the detective answered testily.

"Maybe if you laid off the doughnuts—" Cooper began, but she saw that Stern was in no mood for joking.

"Do you know how stupid it was coming in here alone?" he said.

"I wasn't alone, exactly," Cooper replied. "Elizabeth was here." She turned around, realizing for the first time that Elizabeth had disappeared again.

"The ghost?" the detective said. "I swear, you are the strangest kid I've ever met. Are you telling me a ghost knocked that guy down those steps?"

"It wasn't me," Cooper said. "And Annie is still tied to a chair back there. Which reminds me, we should probably let her go."

They went back into the office, and the detective used a knife to cut the ropes on Annie's hands and feet. When she was free, she jumped up and hugged Cooper tightly.

"I was so scared," she said.

"Me too," Cooper said. "For a minute there I thought I might lose one of my best friends. Not to mention ending up dead myself."

"Did you see this ghost too?" the detective asked Annie.

Annie nodded. "She saved us," she said.

The detective sighed. "Do me a favor, will you?" he said. "Don't mention any of this to that Barclay woman. Let me come up with something."

Cooper grinned. "Only if you let me ride in the patrol car with the sirens going on the way home," she said.

What a weird two weeks this has been, Cooper thought as she lit the candle.

It was Tuesday night, and Cooper was in her bedroom. Normally she would be at her Wicca study group, but a lot had happened since the night before. After reuniting Annie with her aunt, Cooper had had to go home and tell her parents what had happened. They had been furious with her, but once they'd realized she was fine, they'd calmed down. A little. They were still angry at her for doing something so dangerous, and had threatened never to let her leave the house again. But in all the excitement, they hadn't even noticed the damage to the Nash.

As for Annie, her aunt *had* forbidden her to leave the house—except for going to school—at least for a few days. Sarah was constantly asking Annie if she was okay, which was starting to get on Annie's nerves. Kate was the only one who hadn't experienced any fallout from the ordeal of the night before. Luckily for her, as far as her parents knew, she'd spent the whole evening at the movies with Tyler.

But the best part was that the mystery was finally over. After a lot of grilling by Detective

Stern, Dan Huctwith finally admitted to killing Martha Perch, the homeless Johnny, and Elizabeth Sanger—and to setting up Christopher Barrons. An embarrassed district attorney had dropped all charges against Barrons, and he had been freed. Amanda Barclay, equally embarrassed at having fallen for Dan Huctwith's game, wrote a column about how perhaps the state's death penalty wasn't such a good idea if an innocent man could be so easily set up. Reading it, Cooper's father had said, "I still say she's a smart reporter." Then he'd looked at his daughter and added, "But not as smart as some other people I know."

Cooper herself was just glad that Stern had kept her and Annie's names out of the paper. He'd told reporters that he'd acted on a tip and found Dan Huctwith hiding out in the old warehouse. "Let people believe what they want," she told Kate and Annie. "I don't care as long as my phone stops ringing."

Cooper looked at the altar she'd set up in her bedroom. It was just a little table, really, one she'd found in the cellar. She'd set it against the wall beside her desk, so she could look at it when she worked. She'd decided to make her first personal altar because she felt as if she'd completed the first major challenge of her year and a day of study. Helping Elizabeth, and learning how to use her talent for seeing, made her feel more connected to Wicca, and especially to the Goddess. She wanted to do something to symbolize that, and making a place where she could celebrate her relationship with the Goddess, and with Wicca, seemed like a good idea.

She'd asked Sophia and Archer how to make an altar. They'd explained that there were all kinds of altars, and that each one was as personal as the person or people who created it. They'd suggested that she create a space that contained symbols that were important to her or that reminded her of things she was working on in her study of the Craft.

She started by placing a dark red cloth on the table. The red reminded her of fire, which had played such a huge part in her recent experiences. It was in the fire that she'd seen and met Elizabeth. It also reminded her of the Beltane bonfires and of the scarlet ribbons in Thatcher's beard and on the maypole. And it reminded her of Pele, the fiery volcano goddess who had come to her in her dreams.

In the center of the altar she placed a red candle, again to represent fire. On one side of the candle she placed the statue of Pele that Kate had given her. As Sophia had explained, the Goddess came in many forms, and different people preferred to think of her in different ways. Pele was one form of the Goddess, and Cooper liked the statue both because it reminded her of her dreams and her own personality and because it had been given to her by one of her two best friends.

On the other side of the candle she placed the scrying bowl Annie had given her. Not only was it a cherished gift, but it symbolized another of the elements—water—as well as the first of the many challenges she knew she would face on her journey into Wicca. It also symbolized the first of her gifts that she'd learned to use, and Archer told her that keeping the bowl on her altar would be a good way to surround it with the kind of positive energy that she wanted to feel when she used it.

Now that the altar had been set up, Cooper placed the last item on it. It was a picture of Elizabeth Sanger that she'd cut from the newspaper and put into a little frame. Cooper hadn't had a chance to say good-bye to Elizabeth, and she also didn't want to forget her. She liked the idea of having her picture on the altar. She didn't know where Elizabeth's spirit was, but she hoped it was happy and at peace.

She looked at the burning candle and at the various items on her altar. She knew she would add more things as she learned more and experienced more. But at the moment it looked absolutely perfect. She sat on the floor and thought about everything that had happened to her in the previous two weeks. Things with her parents, especially with her mother, were going to be different now that they knew about her involvement with Wicca. She didn't know yet how that would work out. And then there was T.J. But she would think about him later. Right now she wanted to think about Elizabeth. She closed her eyes and pictured the girl's face.

"Elizabeth," she said softly, "wherever you are, I hope you're okay. Thank you for trusting me. Most of all, thank you for teaching me about my gifts."

As if in answer, a breeze blew through her open window and extinguished the candle. Cooper sat in the darkness, looking at the outlines of Pele and the scrying bowl. Then, out of nowhere, a spark lit the darkness and the flame rekindled. Cooper smiled to herself as the candle burned brightly once more.

"Blessed be, Elizabeth," she said. "And merry meet."

with Book 4: what the cards said

Annie adjusted her turban and rearranged the folds of her black velvet robes for what seemed like the thousandth time. The bracelets on her arms jangled softly, and she paused to examine her fingernails, which Kate had spent half an hour painting a deep red. She liked the polish, which she'd never tried before, but she wished she hadn't let Kate convince her not to wear her glasses. She could see things close up, but anything farther away than the ends of her arms started to get blurry. She was just able to make out the entrance to the tent, but it was as if she was looking at everything under water.

She couldn't believe that they had talked her into doing this. What had she been thinking? What if she made a mess of everything? What if nobody even came? *At least then no one will see you looking like some kind of thrift store genie*, she thought, once more pushing back the turban, which kept threatening to slip down over her forehead.

Despite her reservations, she had to admit that she was sort of getting into playing the part of Miss Fortune, Tarot reader and seer into the future. They'd done a great job of setting up her tent for the carnival. The table in front of her was covered with a black cloth, and there were candles flickering in different parts of the tent, filling it with constantly moving shadows. All in all, the mood was very witchy.

It had all been Cooper's idea. Two weeks before, during their weekly Wicca study group at Crones' Circle bookstore, they had been working with Tarot cards. Archer was describing the different cards and their meanings, and Annie had been fascinated by them. She'd been doing a lot of reading about the Tarot on her own, and it was fun to put what she'd learned to use. Archer showed them how to do a simple reading using five cards, and then they'd split into pairs to practice. Annie and Cooper had been partners, and Annie had really gotten into it.

But when Cooper suggested that Annie tell fortunes at the upcoming school carnival, held every year before finals, she'd hesitated. For one thing, she was still getting over the events of the weeks before, when she, Cooper, and Kate had become involved in solving the murder of a girl at school and Annie had been used as a hostage by the girl's killer. Even more important, while she'd practiced with the Tarot cards a lot outside of class, she wasn't at all sure she could read them accurately, especially for other people.

Cooper and Kate worked on her, however, and finally she agreed to give it a try, if only to get her friends off her back. Now, sitting in the tent they'd put up for her and waiting for her first visitor to come inside, she decided that she'd made a terrible mistake, excellent costume or not. She listened to the sounds of the carnival going on outside her tent. There were booths of all kinds set up around the school grounds, and the air was filled with voices as people talked, laughed, and shouted to one another. *Why would any of them come in here?* Annie asked herself. There were so many other things to see and do. Every club, class, and student organization had come up with *something* to do for the carnival, so there was a lot going on. She herself was doing the readings to raise money for a new science lab.

She sat there for fifteen minutes, listening to everyone else having a good time and smelling the scents of popcorn and hot dogs that wafted in on the breeze. Her stomach rumbled, and she thought about how much nicer it would be to be chewing on a sugary sweet cloud of cotton candy and talking to her friends. She was just about to take the irritating turban off and call it quits when she saw the flaps of the tent open and someone came inside. Between the darkness and her bad eyesight, she wasn't sure who it was.

"Welcome," she said, trying her best to sound mysterious but coming across more like she had a bad cold. "I am Miss Fortune. Please sit."

"How very spooky," the person said, walking to the table and dropping into the chair across from Annie. "And what a lovely turban. Very Aladdin."

Any excitement Annie might have been feeling about playing Miss Fortune disappeared as soon as she recognized the voice and saw the familiar face framed by the glow of candlelight. It was Sherrie Adams. Of all the people who could possibly walk through the tent's flaps, why did popular-but-mean Sherrie have to be her first customer? If Annie hadn't been nervous before, she certainly was now. If there was anyone at Beecher Falls High School who would like to see Annie Crandall make a fool of herself, it was Sherrie.

Isobel Bird

join the circle...

Book 1: So Mote It Be

There's practically nothing about February that Kate likes—the only bright spot is Valentine's Day, and even that looks dreary with no likely prospects in sight. So when a love spell crosses her path, what's a girl to do? Little does Kate know that her impulsive decision to cast a spell will have consequences—both good and bad—far beyond what she'd intended.

0-06-447291-4

Book 2: Merry Meet

Joined by an uneasy bond, Kate, Cooper, and Annie are resolved to explore their newfound fascination with witchcraft. The three very different girls attend an open pagan ritual, and while each is drawn to the power of witches, it becomes apparent that they must come together as three before they might begin to learn the ways of Wicca.

0-06-447292-2

Book 4: What the Cards Said

Annie's fascination with tarot spirals beyond her control when her readings become reality. As if cursed, Annie faces friends Cooper and Kate with a power that threatens the very strength of their Wiccan bond.

0-06-447294-9